PIRATES *the* CARIBBEAN
SALAZAR'S REVENGE

BOOK OF THE FILM

PAPER ROCKET
Stories that take you to another world

This edition published 2017 by Paper Rocket
an imprint of Parragon Books Ltd.
Paper Rocket logo and name ™ Parragon Books Ltd

Parragon Books Ltd
Chartist House
15–17 Trim Street
Bath BA1 1HA, UK
www.parragon.com

Written by Jeff Nathanson
Adapted by Greg Ehrbar
Based on Walt Disney's Pirates of the Caribbean
Based on characters created by Ted Elliot, Terry Rossio, Stuart Beattie
and Jay Wolpert

ISBN 978-1-4748-7217-1

Printed in UK

DISNEP

PIRATES of the CARIBBEAN

SALAZAR'S REVENGE

BOOK OF THE FILM

PAPER ROCKET
Stories that take you to another world

PROLOGUE

"LET ME TELL YOU A STORY – A TALE OF THE
GREATEST TREASURE ANY MAN CAN HOLD...."

AS THE FULL MOON POURED THROUGH HIS
window, 12-year-old Henry Turner looked up, a
surge of excitement running through him. It was
time to go. There was no question about it. For
years, he had been poring over his books, delving
deep into the legends of the sea, and now he'd
finally found what he needed.

With a heart squeezed tight in hope, Henry
glanced around his dimly lit room. Well-worn
nautical charts and marked-up maps were spread
across his desk, their curling edges held down
by shells and rocks plucked from the beach, and
scattered on the bed were books with sea creatures
roaring from their open pages. A figure so distorted
by barnacles that he was hardly recognizable as a
man lurched upwards, as though to seize the reader
in his arms.

Amid the clutter of myths and legends, a roguish face stared out from a poster, the bold letters under his disarming smile spelling out *WANTED: Jack Sparrow*. As Henry cinched his belt, getting ready to leave, he glanced at another picture – one of his father, Will Turner.

It had been years since Henry had seen him, but every day he studied the handsome face, looking for echoes of it in his own, and he often confided his secret dreams and fears to it, as though his father could hear him.

"I'm coming, Father," he whispered, his voice determined.

Henry blew out the candle and grabbed a drawing from his wall. In it, the fearsome sea god Poseidon reared above the waves, brandishing his Trident and commanding everything before him.

After one last glance at his father's image, the boy crawled out of the window into the inky-black night. As he scrambled along the tile roof, the moonlight glinted off his goal: the ocean covering the far horizon.

A short while later, a tiny boat bobbed over the waves, with Henry alone at the oars. Beneath him lay the unfathomable depths of the sea, a mystery to even the most learned scholars. Below the surface, mountains loomed and canyons plunged deep into darkness. In this expanse were creatures yet to be discovered – alive or dead – and a priceless treasure that could change his life forever.

Though he was young, Henry was wise for his years – he thought so, anyway. While other kids had pretended to be soldiers, waging battle among the marshes of the island, he had hung around the docks, learning all he could about sailing, and soaking up stories of the sea. He'd collected anecdotes and rumours as though they were jewels, and carefully filed them all away.

However, none of the tales could match his mother's stories of his father. As far as Henry was concerned, no man, living or dead, was as courageous as Will Turner, who had sacrificed everything to save those he loved.

Henry hummed softly as he rowed, the music keeping time for his strokes. "Yo-ho, yo-ho...."

Once he was satisfied he was out far enough – his island home nothing but a blur on the horizon – Henry paused and pulled his oars into the boat, locking them in place. He made his way to a large burlap sack and hefted it over the bow, the heavy rocks inside knocking together with a series of dull thunks.

Sploosh! As the sack dropped overboard, the rope attached to it unwound frantically like a mad dog, the coils whirling closer and closer to the other end – which was fastened to Henry's right leg.

Now he couldn't undo what was about to happen even if he wanted to.

With complete confidence – and a fearless optimism he had inherited from his mother, Elizabeth Swann, who had commanded pirates, escaped from monsters and sailed into and out of the afterlife – Henry took a deep breath and jumped into the murky depths.

Then it was all darkness. As he fell deeper and deeper, the weight of the sack tugging him down, Henry stayed calm, despite his bursting lungs.

Just as his eyes began to close from the lack of air, his feet struck something solid. Rising from the depths, the wooden deck of a ship had intercepted his fall.

Even though he had expected it, Henry was

flooded with relief as the ship sped to the surface. *The faster, the better,* he thought, almost out cold from the loss of oxygen.

An earsplitting charge of spray leaped from the surface as the ship burst into the night sky. Gallons of water were displaced, cascading over the edge of the massive ship and tracing the name etched on its side: the *Flying Dutchman*. Hundreds of wooden planks screamed as they adjusted to the difference in pressure.

Henry lay on the deck, drawing in great gasps, as the figure of a man approached from the shadows.

"Dad...." Henry's voice cracked.

Will Turner stared in disbelief, his face filling with agony as he recognized his son on his dreadful vessel.

"Henry, what have you done?" Will asked. Henry had grown so much since the last time they'd met. Will thought longingly of all the moments he had missed – Henry's first words, first steps – and of all the future moments he would never witness. The only thing Will's future held was death, just like the past 10 years had held.

"I said I'd find you," Henry piped up cheerfully,

moving towards his father.

But Will immediately recoiled. "Stay away from me!" At the hurt expression on Henry's face, his voice softened. "Look at me, Son."

Will stepped into a beam of moonlight. His once handsome features were now encrusted with 10 years of barnacles, algae and small squirming creatures. His gaze was dull from a decade of despair.

Henry didn't flinch. "I don't care," he declared.

Will wanted more than anything to embrace his son. But he knew Henry needed to leave, fast – before, like him, his boy was stuck there forever. "There is no place for you on the *Dutchman*. Go home to your mother –"

"No," Henry interrupted.

Shuffle, shuffle, creak. Rustling reached them from below the deck. The crew of the *Dutchman* were stirring, sensing the life force of Henry.

"They know you're here," Will said, his voice tight. He unsheathed his sword and, with one swipe, cut the rope binding Henry to the sack. "Leave before it's too late."

"I won't. And if you throw me over, I'll come

straight back." Henry lifted his chin, ignoring the slight queasiness in his stomach at the thought of the others on board.

Will threw his arms up in frustration. Why couldn't his son understand? "Don't you see I'm cursed? Condemned to this ship!"

"That's why I'm here," Henry said excitedly. "I think I know a way to break your curse – to free you from the *Dutchman*!"

"Henry, no." Will shook his head, but his son kept right on talking.

"I've read about a treasure – a treasure that holds all the power of the sea. The Trident of Poseidon can break your curse!"

As Will saw the desperation in Henry's face, his instincts took over. He pulled his boy into his arms and held him tight.

"Henry, the Trident can never be found," he said gently. His son needed to abandon his foolish quest before he wound up dead – or worse. "It's not possible. It's just a tale."

"Like the tales of you and Captain Jack Sparrow? He'll help me find the Trident." Henry's voice was defiant.

Will raised his eyebrows at the name. While he had an inexplicable fondness for the pirate captain, the last thing he wanted was for his son to get tangled up with a man who had a knack for getting into never-ending trouble.

"Stay away from Jack," Will warned. "Leave the sea forever, and stop acting like –"

"A pirate?" Henry asked. He couldn't understand why his father wasn't leaping at the chance to be free. Did he not think Henry was up to the task? "I won't stop. You're my father."

No matter what it took, Henry would track down Jack and the Trident. He'd prove to his father that he was brave and clever.

"I'm sorry, Son," Will whispered, wishing he could be the father Henry needed. The best he could do was try to keep Henry safe and far away from the sea. "My curse will never be broken – this is my fate. You have to let me go."

Will glanced over his shoulder, to the door belowdecks. He and Henry were out of time. He took the amulet from around his neck, pressed it into Henry's hands, and guided him to the rail.

"I will always be in your heart. I love you, Son."

Will helped Henry up and over the edge.

Henry took a moment to imprint his father's face – barnacles and all – on his mind. Then he let go of the rail and dived into the water.

Will watched Henry's thin, wiry frame as he reluctantly climbed back onto his rowing boat. The boy still believed in the folly of happy endings. Will hoped his son didn't have to learn the truth as painfully as he had.

The *Flying Dutchman* disappeared back into the sea. As Henry settled into his rowing boat, the glassy ocean surface left no trace of the massive craft. He was alone again.

But he was more determined than ever to free his father from his wretched fate. So instead of humming as he rowed to shore, Henry passed the time by repeating the name of the one he was sure would help him reach his goal: "Captain Jack Sparrow...."

CHAPTER ONE
SEVEN YEARS LATER

THE MIGHTY BRITISH WARSHIP THE *MONARCH* sliced through the waves, its bow cannons booming, as it chased down a much smaller pirate ship. On the outside, the *Monarch* was a man-made wonder to behold. Inside, things weren't quite as impressive. A troop of young soldiers trudged through filthy black bilgewater on the bottom deck, clearing the sludge as fast as they could. The stench was as foul as the labour was brutal.

"Faster, you pathetic bilge rats!" Officer Maddox bellowed from his spot above the soldiers. He strutted along, peering down at the line of men, spittle flying from his mouth as he screamed at them. "You'll pump the bilge and fill the scuppers! We're chasing down pirates!"

Few ships were as well equipped as the *Monarch*. With 100 cannons aboard, no pirate ship stood a chance in a fight. The *Ruddy Rose* had chosen to flee, but the *Monarch* was in hot pursuit.

Henry Turner, now 19, was among the soldiers straining every muscle manning the bilge and scuppers to lend speed to the vessel. He had become used to hard work – and to difficult men like Maddox. As the officer turned his back to scold a new recruit, Henry ducked out of line and peered out of a window, raising a spyglass to his eye.

"*Psst!* Henry!" a fellow soldier whispered. "Get back here. You don't want to be kicked off another ship!"

"It's a Dutch barque," Henry said, ignoring the warning. "Probably stolen by the pirate Bonnet."

"When are you going to give up, Henry?" his friend asked. "You'll never find Jack Sparrow!"

"I'll never give up." Henry's voice was emphatic. Over the years, he'd followed many false leads. Everyone had a story about the notorious pirate, but no one seemed to know where to find him. Henry had joined the British navy – whose main mission seemed to be pirate hunting – in the hope that they would help him track down Sparrow.

As the British ship pivoted in the water, Henry

spotted a strange rock formation ahead. It was an odd sight – a huge archway in the middle of the wide expanse of the sea. Henry knew enough legends to recognize it instantly – and it wasn't good.

"My God," he whispered in dread.

The rogue pirate ship was heading right towards it, retreating from the *Monarch*'s gunfire. Henry had to stop the *Monarch* from following it. Dashing for the stairs, he nearly crashed into Maddox.

"I've warned you about leaving your post, boy! Shall I show you the lash?" The officer planted his fists on his hips and glared at Henry menacingly.

"Sir, I have to speak to the captain." Henry dodged around Maddox, adding, "Be right back!"

The officer blinked in astonishment. There was no "be right back" under his command. But the lieutenant's cries of *"Turner!"* were lost on Henry, who was already topside.

Sprinting along the deck, Henry pushed his way through the soldiers manning the guns and drawing in the sails to reach Captain Toms and Officer Cole, who stood at the ship's wheel, watching triumphantly as the pirates lowered their flag in defeat.

"Chase her down," Captain Toms ordered. "The British navy does not grant surrender to pirates." As the *Ruddy Rose* approached the gate and began to sail through, the captain nodded towards it. "Follow her in."

"No! Don't do it!" Henry yelled. The officers turned to him in disbelief. Who dared challenge the captain's will? Henry rushed to explain, gesturing to the nearby charts. "Sir, look at your charts. We're between three distant points of land with perfect symmetry to the centre. Captain, you're sailing into the Devil's Triangle."

The captain's eyebrows shot up and he began to laugh. "You hear this, men? He believes an old sailor's myth!"

Henry gritted his teeth, annoyed, as the closest soldiers jeered at him dismissively. "Captain, trust in what I say. Ships that sail into the Triangle do not sail out. Change your course."

"You dare to give me orders?" The captain's face was stern, all traces of laughter gone.

"I won't let you kill us all." Henry flung himself at the ship's wheel and began to reverse direction.

Instantly, soldiers sprang upon him. Henry was no stranger to fighting; his fists and elbows jabbed out as he struggled to get free of their grasp. Had the men been without guns, he might have held them off. Instead, he found himself glaring at a dozen gun barrels, ready to fire. At that moment, Maddox ran up to join them, taking aim as well.

Henry held up his hands but stared defiantly as Captain Toms stalked towards him, his cheeks red with anger.

"This is treason!" Captain Toms declared, furiously tearing the sleeves off Henry's coat to mark his sin. "Take him below. We are going in after that ship."

Maddox was only too happy to lead Henry down to the cells himself. "If it was up to me," he said, throwing the young man into a cell belowdecks, "I'd string you up from the highest yardarm."

As Henry tumbled to the hard floor, a scrap of paper flew from his pocket. It slipped across the wooden planks to stop beside the occupant in the next cell – a grizzled man with a fountain of long white hair. Tattoos on his arms identified him as a pirate.

"Jack Sparrow?" the man said, pointing a bony

finger at the face etched on the paper. "I believe he's dead. Buried in an unmarked grave on the isle of Saint Martin."

Henry sighed. If the *Monarch* was heading into the Triangle, they had more pressing things to worry about than the location of an elusive pirate.

* * *

Racing after the *Ruddy Rose*, the *Monarch* passed through a cloud of smoke from its own guns before sailing under the rock archway. A thick mist rose from the sea around them. Captain Toms raised his spyglass and scanned the ocean, looking for the pirate ship. But it was long gone.

The mist swallowed all sound, plunging the crew into an eerie silence compounded by a sudden darkness, as though the Sun's rays could not reach them anymore.

"Sir, there's something in the water," Officer Cole called, pointing below them.

Swirling in the dark sea was the white outline of a skeletal face with a bloodred rose emblazoned next to it – the flag of the pirate ship they'd been pursuing. But what had happened to the pirates?

Where was their ship? Despite the crew's training, a shiver of apprehension ran through them.

"Ship off the bow," Captain Toms called. He'd spotted something large moving towards them through the mist. But as it got closer, the shape became clearer.

"That's no ship, sir. It's a shipwreck," the first officer said, his voice hushed and worried.

In all his years of service to Her Majesty's Royal Navy, the captain had never seen anything so strange. The ship that was sailing towards them could not possibly be sailing at all.

Its skin was torn off and its bone structure exposed – the wooden ribs of its hull open to the elements. Yet not a drop of water penetrated it as it ploughed towards them. This was the *Silent Mary*.

Despite the impossibility of the decimated ship staying afloat, it was charging them in a very aggressive manner. Already on edge, Captain Toms wasn't going to take any risks, and gave the only order he could think of: *"Fire!"*

The full arsenal of the *Monarch* let loose into the darkness, gunfire blazing. Then there was nothing. The mysterious ship seemed to have disappeared as quickly as it had come.

"Sir," said Maddox, "there is nothing out there." But he had spoken too soon, for whatever had been out there was suddenly right in front of them – on board their ship.

"*Aaaieeeee!*" Screams from the top deck pierced the eerie quiet. Then they cut off abruptly and the only sound was that of footsteps approaching the main deck.

Someone – some*thing* – was coming for them.

Terrified beyond their worst nightmares, the crew pushed towards the walls, recoiling from some invisible menace. Blinded by sweat, they looked to the stairs, waiting to see their enemy.

Instead, a pair of hands shot straight through the wall and grabbed hold of a soldier. His gun and sword clattered to the floor and he was dead before he could utter a word. His fellow soldiers spun uselessly as dozens of arms reached through solid wood as if it were made of pudding.

Disembodied limbs lifted the men, flinging them through the air or snapping their necks. The intruders materialized, looking like monsters from a nightmare. Swords clanged and lanterns were knocked over during the struggle, igniting the ship.

In minutes, a new ghastly crew had taken over. The decks were strewn with bodies and flames. Through the blaze strode the leader of the ghoulish killers, his boots unaffected by the fire.

Reflecting the flames, a chestful of medals glinted from the tattered Spanish navy uniform of Captain Armando Salazar. He casually stepped over soldiers as he headed towards the lone man still standing on the deck.

Captain Toms hid his fear as the dark, hulking form wielding a metre-long sword stopped in front of him. With no apparent effort, Captain Salazar lifted the man into the air.

Captain Toms abandoned his bravery and his mouth dropped open in horror at the rotted image before him. The flesh of his assailant's face was crisscrossed by black lines, and the left side of his head was missing a large chunk.

"What *are* you?" Captain Toms asked.

"Death," Salazar replied, thrusting his sword through Toms's heart.

Dropping his victim to the floor, Captain Salazar spun to address his crew. "Return those pokers and remove your caps!" he barked.

"You heard the captain!" said Officer Lesaro, Salazar's lieutenant. "Order to the front!"

As they snapped to attention, Salazar inspected his ghoulish men. They were not transparent, as ghosts are usually imagined. They were solid beings, their feet on the ground. But dozens of wounds festered on their faces, which were a ghastly grey and covered in black cracks and crevices. Their uniforms had been long rotted and nibbled by vermin, and gaping holes in their bodies allowed one to see straight through to the rails behind them. Once they removed their caps, their hair floated up as though they were underwater.

"By rule of the king, we have provided a fair and just punishment. This ship dared to cross our bow ... and so she will rest at the bottom of the sea," said Salazar, adjusting the collar of a soldier who was missing half his throat. "For years we have been condemned to the Triangle, waiting to escape the borders that confine us. I assure you, my very dead men, your loyalty will be rewarded with blood, as we will not rest until we have our revenge!"

Trapped in his cell belowdecks, Henry had seen

the ghost ship approach through the porthole. He'd heard the terrors above, caught the flickering shadows of the fight on deck. And he'd tried to remain as still and silent as possible.

But in the cell next door, the old pirate stretched out his hand, catching drops of blood oozing from the slats above him. Henry could not stop him from screaming. Alerted, the ghosts began reaching through the prison walls. And then the old man screamed no more.

Creak, creak.

Captain Salazar advanced down the stairs and towards Henry's cell. Then he stepped right through the bars. Henry backed up to the ship's wall, his pulse racing.

Captain Salazar paused, the sheet of paper with Jack Sparrow's portrait catching his eye.

"Do you know this pirate?" asked Salazar, spearing the parchment with his sword and raising it high.

Henry swallowed nervously. "Only in name," he said.

Captain Salazar pinned him with his sharp eyes, alight with interest. "Are you looking for him?"

"Yes," Henry croaked.

Captain Salazar felt his luck had finally turned. Jack Sparrow and the compass he'd stolen held the key to releasing Salazar and the *Silent Mary* from the cursed Triangle.

"No need to fear me, boy," Captain Salazar drawled. "I always leave one man alive to tell the tale. Now, go find Sparrow for me – and relay this message from Captain Salazar: on the day I behold daylight again, I will come straight for him!"

A raw, throaty cheer rose from Salazar's crew as dozens of questions swirled through Henry's mind: How did Captain Salazar know Jack Sparrow? What had Jack done to anger him? How would Henry find Jack? With a vengeful bunch of ghosts on their tail, could they hope to find the Trident and free Henry's father?

The captain leaned almost nose to nose with Henry. "I'd tell him myself," he continued, "but dead men tell no tales."

CHAPTER TWO

CARINA SMYTH DARTED THROUGH THE CROWD of well-dressed citizens on the busy street of Saint Martin, her blue dress swishing and the metal links of a chain around her left wrist clanking as she ran.

"Stop that witch!" a voice behind her cried.

The young woman would have rolled her eyes, but she was too busy searching for an escape from the quartet of soldiers pursuing her. Why did men always confuse knowledge with witchcraft when it came to women? She was a scholar of science and the stars.

She had been fascinated by astronomy ever since she was a little girl, in honour of a father she'd never met. The only link she had to him was a weathered diary, its pages inscribed with mathematical formulas and charts of the sky. She'd been in search of the map it referenced for years, and she wasn't about to let some simpleminded soldiers stop her, which was precisely why she'd picked the lock of her cuffs and escaped the cell they'd tossed her into.

Suddenly, a young soldier blocked her way, his nervous expression betraying his fear of the supposed witch. Without hesitating, Carina spun past him and dived under a wagon, then rolled out the other side and disappeared into the ever-growing crowd.

The soldiers gave up and turned back to report to their leader, Lieutenant John Scarfield. Clearly she'd used her magic to vanish, and there was nothing they could do about it. But their furious commander saw things differently.

"You're telling me four of my men have lost one girl?" he growled. The officer's face was flushed, and his broad shoulders were bunched tight. He gritted his teeth in frustration.

At that stage of his career, he should have been in command of his own fleet, fighting wars in West Africa, not stuck on that humid island, hunting down witches. It was taking too long, clawing his way up through the British navy, but what could he do when he was saddled with incompetents like this?

"Find me that wicked lass or you'll swing in her place!" he snarled at his pathetic troops before stalking off.

His men pushed through the crowd gathering in front of the bank, searching the faces for the witch. But all they found were the excited townsfolk jostling for a better view.

That day was the unveiling of the Royal Bank of Saint Martin, and they were eager to see the new marvel that would safeguard the wealth of the island.

The portly figure of Mayor Dix stood before the bank, a proud smile on his face, as he introduced its features to the townsfolk. If there had ever been a bigger day in his career, he couldn't remember it. It was he who had argued for the bank's construction, insisted on the finest materials, and approved the budget for an expensive robbery-proof safe. Now all those endless days and nights of meetings, design and supervision would be worth it.

"Ladies and gentlemen, with this bank, the

town of Saint Martin enters the modern world," proclaimed Mayor Dix as the bank doors were opened.

The crowd gasped at the sight of the imposing metal box in the centre of the room. Hundreds of Sunday-best shoes shuffled as folks moved forward to get a better look, and several people remarked about the "new bank smell".

"Our new vault is five inches thick, stands as tall as any man, and weighs an imperial ton," explained Mayor Dix as he took his place on the steps before it. "No man could ever rob such a vault!"

At the mayor's nod, the band, which had been rehearsing for weeks, began to play. In perfect time to the music, the bank manager, Mr Krill, opened the huge door of the safe. His back to the vault, the mayor made a grand "Ta-da!" gesture.

The music slowed to a halt, the band members dropping their instruments to their sides. Townspeople murmured in confusion. The mayor heard the loud rumbling of someone snoring behind him. Slowly, he turned to see what was causing the commotion.

Lying across the top shelf inside the vault and

covered head to toe in gold coins was Jack Sparrow.

"Pirate!" a woman in the crowd screamed, startling Jack awake.

"Pirate!" Jack shouted in alarm, echoing the lady. From his dazed state, it was obvious that he'd had plenty from the jug of rum in his hand.

Jack rolled to the ground in a shower of gold coins and blinked at his audience. Who were those people who'd awakened him so rudely? What were they doing on his ship? More importantly, had they brought more rum?

When Jack figured out his swaying was caused by the rum in his hands rather than the floor beneath him, he realized he must be on land. Knocking his hand against the floor, he discovered it was made of metal. Pieces of the puzzle began to come to him. He was in a bank vault – one of the easiest he'd ever broken into. Now he just had to remember what he was doing there.

"This may seem a peculiar request," Jack began, gazing blearily at the guards taking aim at him, "but would someone kindly remind me as to why I'm here?"

"Hold your fire!" one of the soldiers commanded.

"There's a woman in there with him!"

Indeed, a red-haired woman with her clothes in disarray had just sat up next to Jack.

"He can't hide behind that trollop!" Mayor Dix snapped.

"Sir," said an embarrassed Mr Krill, "I believe that's your wife."

"Frances?" The mayor's voice rose in astonishment as the woman tugged up her sleeves and smoothed her hair away from her face.

Glancing down at his feet, Jack spotted thick ropes that ran under the vault and through holes bored into the back of it. He frowned, peering outside. Jack could make out his faithful crew members Gibbs and Scrum tying the ropes to their wagons. Filling out the motley group were Marty, Pike, Bollard and Cremble. Three teams of horses were at the ready.

"Right," Jack said to himself as the ropes by his feet began to tighten. "Got it. I'm robbing the bank."

"Shoot him!" ordered the mayor.

Mrs Dix beat a hasty retreat and Jack dived for cover as bullets riddled the pristine vault walls.

"Not the bank, just the pirate!" Mayor Dix cried.

Hearing the shots, the horses whinnied in fear and heaved against their ropes, pulling the vault from its position. It slid across the bank floor.

WHAM!

The vault hit the back wall of the bank. It might have stayed there if the guards had not fired again, sending the horses into complete panic. Their strength and terror caused them to break the bank – literally. Thin supports surrounding the building gave way like slivers.

Jack got to his feet, trying to find his sea legs in the open doorway of the bank as it began to shake and fall apart.

Standing fully exposed, Jack faced the guns again. "This was not part of the plan," he murmured.

One of the ropes caught his ankle. The bank rumbled and groaned. It was leaving, and taking Jack with it. Swept off his feet, Jack was hauled along behind the runaway vault.

"He's stealing the bank!" cried the mayor, spurring the guards to give chase.

Choked by dirt and debris, Jack managed to spin around and start to pull himself up the rope towards the mobile bank – just in time to see hundreds of gold coins pouring from the vault. Eyes wide, Jack tried to grab them as they bounced past him. The townsfolk, who were following the runaway bank, had better luck as they snatched up the riches spilling down the street.

Spying an awning extending from the bank, Jack jumped up and grabbed on, shaking the rope around his boot loose. He was barely able to hang on as the pirates urged the horses forward and the bank careened faster and faster through the town.

The horses turned sharply around a corner, smashing half the bank against another building. Jack ducked splinters of wood as the walls crashed and crumbled. Losing his grip on the awning, Jack flew through a window, then sailed past a family sitting down to eat and right out another window.

"Oof!" Jack landed back on the street, but as he staggered to his feet, he saw that the vault – and the Royal Guard – were ahead of him.

Two of the soldiers glanced back and shouted in surprise to see him behind them, but before they could fire, the bank crashed into a shop, the noise distracting them. When the soldiers turned back to aim at the pirate, he was already gone.

Oblivious to the chaos in the streets outside, Carina Smyth peered through a telescope at Swift and Sons Chart House, making adjustments to its dials. Mr Swift, the proprietor of the shop, gasped in horror when he saw her there.

"No woman has ever handled my telescope!" he exclaimed, his nostrils flaring.

"Sir, your celestial fix was off. I've adjusted it two degrees north so your maps will no longer be imprecise. Although, you will have to start over with these." Carina motioned towards dozens of maps that hung on the walls, which had taken the not-so-swift Mr Swift decades to draw up.

Unaffected by her beauty and wary of her cleverness, the flustered shopkeeper noted the dirt on Carina's face and the broken chain dangling from her wrist. There could be but one explanation.

"You're a witch," he said.

Here we go again, she thought. "Sir, I am no witch," said Carina. "I simply need to purchase a chronometer. I'll pay you double for selling to a woman."

She held aloft the chronometer she desired and reached for her purse. But Mr Swift would not aid a witch, let alone a fugitive.

"Help!" he cried, pulling out a gun and aiming it at her with shaking hands. "There's a witch in my shop!" he screamed.

Jack sprinted into the chart house. Now Swift wasn't sure where to aim.

"And a pirate!" Jack added helpfully. He thought for a moment. "And a bank," he said, pulling Carina away from the walls just as the bank crashed into Swift and Sons, cutting it in half.

The spot where Carina had been standing was destroyed. Swift stared at his demolished shop in dismay.

Crash. His beloved telescope toppled to the floor.

Jack and Carina dashed away in the confusion. Out on the streets, they were quickly spotted by both the Royal Guard and Scarfield's men, so they ducked down an alley.

The guards and soldiers stopped in front of a shop window, having lost their quarry. They were so busy scanning the streets that they didn't notice two formally dressed display mannequins had familiar heads – Jack's and Carina's.

"Were you part of the plan?" Jack asked Carina

curiously.

"I'm not looking for trouble," Carina replied out of the corner of her mouth.

"What a horrible way to live," Jack muttered.

"I need to escape," Carina continued. "Can you help me?"

"That man called you a witch, and witches are bad luck at sea," Jack said, somewhat regretfully.

"We're not at sea," she countered.

"Good point. But I am a pirate," Jack said. He might as well carry the sea with him.

"But I am clearly not a witch."

"One of us is very confused." Jack cocked his head as he considered the young brunette.

"By all appraisals, that would be you." She knew exactly who she was and what sort of man stood before her.

Jack's brow furrowed. "Would you excuse me?" he said. "I seem to have misplaced a bank."

Dodging gunfire, the two bolted from their hiding place and climbed to a rooftop. Below them they could see the soldiers and guards circling, but there were no ladders or nearby buildings they could reach.

"We're trapped. What do we do?" Carina asked, whirling towards Jack.

"*You* need to scream," said Jack calmly, pushing Carina off the building.

"*Aaaah!*" Carina was forced to oblige as she plummeted through the air. But instead of crashing to the street, she landed, unhurt, on top of a wagon filled with soft straw. "Filthy pirate," she shouted after him.

As Jack had planned, the soldiers took off after the wagon, giving him the chance to get back to robbing the bank. Jack ran towards a flagpole and used it to vault off the roof and back onto the bank just as it sped past. With quick steps, he scrambled up the side as the tiles dropped off beneath him.

But Jack's timing could not have been worse. The horses were about to gallop under a stone bridge – a bridge both he and the bank could not pass beneath.

"Bridge ... *Bridge! Stop, horses!*" Jack bellowed, but his crew could not hear him, and the horses paid him no mind.

Jack jumped up onto the bridge and sprinted across the top as the horses headed under it. The bank blasted into the bridge, but the opening was not large enough for the walls to fit through.

It was, however, just the right height for the vault to be forced out the other side. Jack leaped into the air and landed on top of the safe as the horses dragged it away from the town. The Royal Guard pulled up short at the bridge, trapped behind the bank debris, which clogged the only opening out of town.

The few townspeople who had not gone home to hide clustered in front of what was left of the bank. Their town's shiny new building lay in unrecognizable ruins.

The bank sign dropped to the ground in front of Mayor Dix as he stepped over the remnants of his hopes for Saint Martin's future and prosperity. All his hard work and dreams had been undone by a wretched pirate.

Preoccupied by their misfortune, nobody noticed a lithe woman clothed in a blue dress and manacle who stood among them, surveying the scene.

Having used her as a distraction, Jack and his cohorts had made it out of town. *Good riddance,* she thought. *He wreaks havoc yet seems to come out ahead.*

And they call me *a witch.*

CHAPTER THREE

THE STOLEN BANK VAULT STOOD ON THE DECK of Captain Jack's small, dilapidated ship, the *Dying Gull*. It hadn't been easy for the crew to hoist the heavy thing on board. Jack was exhausted just from leaning against the deck, pointing his index finger here and there to direct the crew in carrying and placement of the vault.

The well-worn wooden slats of the deck strained under the vault's considerable weight. Once it was placed to his liking, Jack carefully reached inside and took out the spoils of their crime: a single coin. The rest had fallen out during the chase. The crew glared at him.

"I told you robbing a bank would be easy," Jack said breezily. For it was true: they *had* robbed the bank with great success. That the gold was no longer inside the vault was a technicality. "Now line up to offer your tribute, men!"

Marty put his fists on his hips and cocked his bald head. "You want *us* to pay *you*?" he asked. "We want our treasure, Captain! The treasure you've been promising us all these years!"

"All of us are starving," Pike said mournfully. "Yesterday we ate a rat."

"We will no longer follow a captain without a ship!" Bollard exclaimed, planting his feet wide and gesturing to the ramshackle boat they stood on, more a barge than a ship, and one that happened to be beached on a thin strip of land.

Jack sniffed, insulted. The *Dying Gull* was a little worse for wear, but it was seaworthy – or it would be as soon as the crew patched it up. And besides, Jack had a *grand* vessel, as well – the greatest ship of all that travelled the high seas.

"I have a ship, gentlemen," he said dramatically, opening his coat and reaching in. "The *Black Pearl* has never left my side!"

Jack pulled out a glass bottle and held it up high. Inside, the *Black Pearl* rested, a fraction of its original size.

Pike leaned back, unimpressed. "The pirate Barbossa rules these seas now," he said. "He has ten ships, guns full."

The rest of the crew began to grumble as well and head towards the gangplank.

"Wait!" said Jack, holding up his hand to stop them from leaving. "Did we not find the Treasure of Macedonia together?"

Gibbs looked up and sighed. "It was a trove of rotted wood!"

Jack tried again. "But the gold of King Midas –"

"Was a steaming pile of cow dung," finished Scrum, the scene still fresh in his mind.

"Face it, Jack," Gibbs said, his expression sad. "Bad luck follows you day and night."

"Bad luck? Ridiculous!" Jack blustered just as a passing seagull deposited its droppings on his shoulder.

"We know you fear your own sword," Scrum spoke. "That you believe it's cursed – with the intention of slitting your throat!"

Jack grimaced. They had a point there. The sword seemed to have a mind of its own – a mind that hated him. He sauntered over to the dreaded weapon, picked it up and flung it into the sea, as if it were a piece of stale bread.

"Problem solved," he said, brushing off his hands on his breeches. His attempt to assume a cool, casual attitude did not fool his men. They knew him too well.

"You've lost your luck, your ship, and now your crew," said Marty.

Unwilling to follow Jack any longer, the men walked away. Gibbs was the last to go, gazing at Jack regretfully.

"Sir," the grizzled man said, "I'm afraid we've reached the end of the horizon."

Jack looked down at his compass, which was pointing out to sea. "They're wrong, Gibbs," he replied. "I am still Captain Jack Sparrow."

"If you say so, Jack." Gibbs fiddled with his cap. "Good luck."

Jack's face twisted in a sneer and he flounced to the far side of the boat, not wanting to watch his men abandon him. He set the bottle on the rail and squatted down until the *Black Pearl* looked like it was resting on the edge of the sea. His men lacked vision, but Jack could see it. The *Pearl* would sail again, and he would be, as ever, its captain.

* * *

The military hospital of Saint Martin was bustling with activity. Soldiers lay with varying degrees of injury, their moans and cries filling the air, summoning nuns to their sides.

Henry Turner winced at a twinge in his neck as he slowly awoke, startled by the strange sounds and smells around him. Then three soldiers loomed over him, one of them wearing the stripes of a lieutenant.

Officer Scarfield twisted his hands tightly around the bed rail. "The whole town speaks of you – the only survivor of the *Monarch*," he said, his voice cool. "A boy who paddled all the way to Saint Martin on a piece of driftwood and was found jabbering about pirates and tridents."

Henry tried to sit up, but heavy shackles trapped him firmly to the bed.

"Sir, release me from these chains. I have to find Captain Jack Sparrow," Henry pleaded.

"Your sleeves have been ripped – the mark of treason," Scarfield continued, his voice full of disgust.

"We were attacked by the dead, sir," Henry explained. "I tried to warn them!"

Scarfield shook his head, unmoved. "You're a coward who ran from battle. And that is how you will die."

Turning on his heel, Scarfield led his men away, leaving Henry to sigh in dejection. Would his quest end there?

A nun approached his bed and held a cup of water out to him.

"I don't believe you are a coward," she said.

"Please leave me, Sister," Henry said softly. It was kind of the sister to try to comfort him, but all he wanted was to be alone with his thoughts.

"I've risked my life to come here," the nun said in a rushed whisper, "to see if you truly believe as I believe ... that the Trident will be found."

Henry's gaze flew to the nun in surprise, and he really saw her for the first time. Her blue eyes pinned him to the spot, her expression intense and focused. She was young, beautiful and, judging by the torn dress peeking beneath her habit and the iron cuff around her wrist, not a nun at all.

"Tell me why you seek the Trident," Carina

urged him as she glanced over her shoulder. She didn't have much time.

Henry shook his head to clear it, sensing that his answer held great importance to her. "The Trident can break any curse at sea," he explained. "My father is trapped by such a curse."

The young woman's eyebrow shot up in scepticism. "You're aware of the fact that curses are not supported by science?"

"Neither are ghosts," Henry answered, his voice laden with certainty.

"So you have gone mad, as I had heard." Carina frowned and began to stand up. "The laws of modern science —"

"Have nothing to do with the myths of the sea," Henry interjected. How could she concede the existence of the Trident of Poseidon but not believe in the possibility of curses or ghosts? "Why did you come here?"

"I need to get off this island to solve the Map No Man —" Carina began.

"Can Read," Henry finished in awe. She was searching for the same treasure as he.

"So you've read the ancient texts," Carina said.

"In each language they were written," Henry answered enthusiastically. He couldn't believe he'd found another person who knew about the Map No Man Can Read. "The map was left behind by Poseidon himself. But no man has ever seen it."

"Luckily, I'm a woman," said Carina, producing an ancient diary from beneath her nun's robe. The brown leather of the volume was cracked by the passage of time. On the cover, a red ruby was embedded over a sea of embossed stars.

"This is the diary of Galileo Galilei. He spent his life looking for the map. It's why he invented the spyglass – why astronomers have spent their lives looking to the sky." She ran her fingers over the cover, then flipped through the worn yellowed pages covered in diagrams of constellations and notations of the phases of the moon.

Henry's brow creased. "You're saying the Map No Man Can Read is hidden in the stars?"

"Yes, but I have yet to see it," she answered.

"Just because you can't see something doesn't mean it isn't there," he said. He'd encountered enough supernatural phenomena to know that truth well.

Carina bit her lip, wondering if the odd young man could really help her. He did not have a scientific mind, to be sure, but perhaps his knowledge of the lore of the sea would come in handy.

"This diary was left to me by my father," she explained. "He believed I could find what no man has ever found, and I will not let him down. Soon there will be a blood moon." Carina stopped on a page with a drawing of a cluster of five stars in a sea of black and white dots and showed it to Henry. "Only then will the map be read – and the Trident found."

"Who are you?" Henry wondered aloud as the young woman produced a pick and began to unlock his chains.

"Carina Smyth!" someone snarled.

Carina froze, knowing if she turned, she'd find Scarfield and his men behind her.

Pressing the pick into Henry's hands, she hissed, "If you wish to save your father, you'll have to save me. Find us a ship, and the Trident will be ours."

Scarfield drew his sword. "Turn to me, witch!" he commanded.

Carina pushed away from the hospital bed,

which offered her just the leverage she needed to shove Scarfield and his men aside. She wove around nuns and past beds, her flowing robe flapping like a ship's sail.

Just inches from the doorway to freedom, Carina's path was blocked by Scarfield and his men.

Carina held her chin high as she faced the men.

"Sir," one of the soldiers gasped, pointing behind her, "he's gone!"

Everyone whirled to see that Henry's bed was empty, his shackles piled on the sheets. The wind silently ruffled the curtains at a nearby open window.

Carina's eyes were clear as she gazed at the sky, but hope and dread warred in her chest. Now her fate lay in the hands of a stranger, a young man who believed in ghosts and curses, but one whose loyalty to his father might be her salvation.

CHAPTER FOUR

JACK SPARROW CROUCHED LOW AMONG shrubbery flanking a lonely highway. Now that he'd lost his crew, he could not command a ship at sea. Therefore, he'd decided he would pillage, plunder and loot on land.

What good was a crew anyway if they deserted him when things were a little off? "They dare to call me cursed," he muttered, "as riches forge my way on land!"

A coach jangled towards him. Gold filigree highlighted the hand-carved details of the carriage, and even the horses wore decorations. Even better, a pair of powdered wigs was clearly visible through the windows. There would be prime pickings inside.

Jack leaped from behind the bushes and struck a dramatic pose. He had been rehearsing since that morning and settled on his present stance as the most threatening and imposing.

"Today," he declared boldly, "you will be robbed by Jack the Highwayman! As my luck returns —"

Before Jack could finish his speech, the coach whisked by and headed towards town. The dust it kicked up covered him from head to foot, as though mocking him.

It could be worse, he thought. In seconds, a cold, hard rain began to fall. *Well, now maybe it couldn't.*

The torrential rain continued as Jack re-entered the town of Saint Martin. Protected by awnings and umbrellas, vendors displayed their wares. Jack's eyes sparkled at the sight of barrels of rum, ready to be tapped.

Checking his pockets, he found nothing. He was about to swipe an apple from a stand when soldiers appeared across the square. More soldiers were approaching behind him.

Quickly, Jack threw himself over the nearest fence. A dozen well-fed pigs grunted with indignation as he landed squarely in their mud. Being a highwayman was exhausting. He briefly considered having a nice lie-down in the mud, but the urge for rum was greater and the pigs didn't look very friendly.

Covered in gooey brown mud and in serious need of a drink, Jack entered the nearest pub and staggered up to the bar.

Grimes, the bartender, refused to serve him until Jack showed him some money.

Eternally optimistic, Jack checked his pockets again, just in case. Unfortunately, he didn't have any rogue coins or jewels. The only thing he had to his name, besides the bottle holding the *Black Pearl*, was his trusty compass. He hesitated. The compass had steered him through many dangerous waters and led him to adventure. But what good was a compass when one didn't have a ship or a crew?

Just then a fishing net slammed down on the bar from out of nowhere. Jack saw something familiar sticking out of one of the fish.

"Would you look at that?" the elated fisherman said to Grimes. "A fish stabbed itself with this here sword! I'll sell it to the navy! How's that for luck?"

Before Grimes could reply, Jack slapped his hand on his infernal sword and flung it across the room, trying to remove it from his life yet again. But this time, the tip of the sword speared a wanted poster of him on the wall.

Enough was enough. Jack was going to have that drink, no matter what it cost. He placed the compass on the bar as payment.

"The bottle," he said to Grimes.

The compass quivered, ever so slightly, as it rested on the wooden counter. The movement was just enough to make both of them freeze. Then, behind the bar, all the bottles began to vibrate in unison. A tremor seemed to pass through the pub. In that instant, Jack realized he had made a grave mistake, and he reached to take back the compass.

But it was too late. Grimes grabbed it, handing Jack a bottle of rum in return before tossing the compass onto a pile of gaudy jewellery and cheap trinkets that other desperate men had used as barter for drink.

Jack lifted the bottle he had bought with the compass. He paused before drinking. "A pirate's life," he toasted quietly.

Neither man noticed that the needle on the compass moved again. Miles away, on the deck of the ghostly *Silent Mary*, the ship's wheel rotated by itself – in the same direction as the needle.

The living corpses of dead seagulls circled high above the mast of the *Silent Mary* as the ghostly crew below dutifully scrubbed every nook and cranny of the deck, even though nothing ever became clean. But as the wheel began to spin, the men stopped and stared.

"Sir, what's happening?" Lieutenant Lesaro asked.

Captain Salazar crossed the deck, watching in anticipation as the wheel aimed the ship towards a distant horizon.

"Jack Sparrow has given away the key," he said, moving eagerly to the rail.

The highest peak of the Devil's Triangle began to crumble, revealing a long shaft of light that illuminated the decaying faces of Salazar and his crew. The Triangle started to fall apart, sending rocks tumbling to the sea.

"After all these years, it's time." Captain Salazar's voice was triumphant as daylight danced across his cheeks.

As the Triangle fell, the intense beam of light began to expand. Wider and wider it grew, until there was a blinding burst, enveloping the skeletal

Silent Mary in its glow.

"Hard to starboard," the captain ordered. "We'll sail to the edge and cross with the light!" As the men hastened to obey, a thrill ran through Salazar. "The Triangle will not hold us any longer," he intoned.

Faster and faster, the ship skimmed away from its dank prison, the light guiding it to freedom. Hauling on the ropes, the crew channelled more speed from the ship as it neared the gateway.

The crew braced for impact, but the ship shot out of the crumbling arch with the force of a geyser. Once outside their tomb, the crew paused and looked around. The seas were calm, a bright blue sky stretching overhead.

"We're free!" they cheered.

Captain Salazar stretched his withered arms wide, as if to embrace the new day.

"My very dead men, the sea is ours!" he said, addressing the elated crew. His eyes narrowed on the horizon. "It is time to hunt a pirate! I'll sink every ship at sea until I find and kill Jack Sparrow."

CHAPTER FIVE

UNAWARE OF THE DANGER SAILING TOWARDS him, Jack stumbled out of the bar, bottle in hand. He pulled out the cork to finish it off, but a shot rang out. The bullet hit the bottle, shattering it in his hand and spilling the remaining drops on the ground.

More annoyed than alarmed, Jack turned to find Mayor Dix and a group of soldiers in the street, their weapons fixed on him.

"Just the man we've been looking for," Mayor Dix said with a wry, toothy smile.

"Always nice to be wanted," Jack drawled.

The mayor ignored him and raised his voice as if giving a speech to the passersby, "Let it be known: the pirate Jack Sparrow will be executed at dawn!"

"Executed? That's it – I'll never come here again!" Jack tossed his head in indignation.

But he could do nothing as the soldiers surrounded him and led him away.

* * *

Carina made calculations on the wall of her prison cell as the deep bloodred moon shone through the window. *Why do people insist on being ignorant?* she wondered as she drew a diagram and compared it to one in the diary. *Why do they cling to superstition and fear when science holds the answers?* She supposed it was easier for them to call her a witch than to try to understand. But because of their stupidity, she was trapped in a cell while the blood moon was out. She'd hoped that young soldier, Henry Turner, would find a way to free her before then. But for all she knew, he was miles away.

He did seem to have the same passion, the same drive, for solving the question of the map. True, he believed in fairy tales, just like those who'd locked her up, but while many people she'd met had been preoccupied with their day-to-day routines, Henry had seemed genuinely motivated to do something bigger with his life.

She finished her work on the wall and sighed. She was no closer to finding the truth of the map. She started to close the diary, but then noticed the ruby casting an odd shadow on part of the cover. Henry's words came to mind: *Just because you can't see something doesn't mean it isn't there.* Maybe there was more science in that statement than she had thought.

She dislodged the ruby from the cover and peered through it. The light of the blood moon shining through the ruby revealed writing on the cover that had never been visible before: *To release the power of the sea, all must divide.*

Then she noticed a small drawing that had appeared underneath the constellation on the cover.

"It's an island!" Carina declared. "The stars lead to an island."

Now if only she had a ship – and a way out of the cell before the nonsensical witchcraft accusations got her killed.

* * *

A level below her, Jack sat in a prison cell of his

own, downcast. He missed his crew, his rum and his past good fortune. Food would have been nice, too. *Such a nasty run of luck should not be happening to such a pleasant, agreeable chap,* he thought. Then again, he'd got out of worse situations. He settled in. He might as well take a nap until a solution presented itself.

Several red-coated guards stood down the hall from Jack's cell. Caught up in their own conversation, they didn't notice Henry, disguised as a guard, creeping down the hallway.

His heart beating fast, Henry paused in front of Jack's cell, picking out the shape of a pirate's hat outlined against the window. Henry knew the Royal Guard had arrested Jack Sparrow; now he just had to find him. He hoped this pirate would be able to give him the information he needed.

Leaning close, he whispered, "I need to speak with you."

A hand shot out and grabbed hold of Henry by the neck, pulling him against the bars.

"Hand me your sword," Jack demanded, his voice low and threatening.

"I have no weapon," Henry admitted, nearly

gagging on the ripe, alcoholic smell wafting off the pirate.

"Then you're not a very good soldier," Jack said, silently cursing his continuing bad luck.

"I'm currently wanted for treason," Henry continued. "I've come to see the pirate Jack Sparrow."

Jack released Henry and cocked his head, examining the youth as Henry caught his breath.

"I just happen to be Captain Jack Sparrow," he said. Jack paused, waiting for the fellow to gush with adulation.

Henry was overcome with horror. "No – it can't be," he said, his head spinning. "I've spent years searching for *this*?" He shook his head, refusing to believe it. "The great Jack Sparrow is not some drunk in a cell! What happened to your ship, your crew? Are you sure you're *the* Jack Sparrow?"

"We both know who I am," said Jack, irritated by the lad's reception. "The question remains, who are you?"

"My name is Henry Turner. Son of Will Turner and Elizabeth Swann."

"*Ecch!*" Jack recoiled. The lad's attitude suddenly made more sense. "So you are the evil spawn of those two? He's a cursed fool. She's golden-haired, stubborn, with pouty lips and a neck like a giraffe.... What does she say about me?"

"She never spoke of you," Henry replied, frowning.

Jack harrumphed, absorbing that news. He was surprised to feel a little pang of some emotion, too foreign to identify.

Henry tried to redirect the pirate's attention, knowing he had little time. "Now, I need you to listen, Jack, because at the moment, you're all I've got. I found a way to save my father."

Henry breathlessly told Jack about figuring out that the Trident of Poseidon could end his father's curse and that Carina Smyth could lead them to its site with the Map No Man Can Read. He tried to entice Jack with the idea of the power the Trident held – convince him that it could restore him to his former glory. Then he realized Jack was asleep.

"I'm sorry," Jack slurred, opening one eye. "Were you still talking? I believe I nodded off."

Henry clenched his fists in frustration. Jack was not at all what he'd been expecting. Perhaps this was an imposter. But no, this was the exact face he knew so well from the wanted poster.

Turning to leave, Henry realized he had left out one important detail. Maybe it would be enough to get Jack to cooperate.

"There is one other thing," Henry said. "A message from someone you know. A captain named ... Salazar."

Jack tried to hide it, but Henry could see the jolt that ran through the pirate at the name.

"Him," Jack said, trying to stay calm. "No, no. Quite happily, he's dead. Very, very dead. His ship went down."

"Yes, inside the Devil's Triangle," Henry explained. "He's coming for you, Jack, to seek revenge as the dead man's tale is told. He said your compass was the key to his escape."

Jack's face paled and his hand went instinctively to the pocket where he used to keep the compass. Henry saw the gesture and the flat panel of fabric.

"An army of the dead are coming straight for you, Jack." He looked the pirate right in the eye. This was it; if this didn't convince Jack Sparrow to help him, he didn't know what he would do. "The Trident of Poseidon is your only hope. Do we have an accord?"

"All right then, no need to shout," said Jack, rubbing his throbbing head. "You got any silver?"

CHAPTER SIX

IT WAS SAID THAT BEING A PIRATE WAS LIKE being in a very unique club. A lot of the scallywags had met before – and, more than likely, had crossed swords. All pirates knew better than to trust a fellow buccaneer. Betrayal was so common one didn't need a dagger to stab another in the back.

Yet a few pirates had a strange bond that drew them together. Fate kept uniting them – whether they liked it or not. Such was the case with Jack Sparrow and Hector Barbossa. They shared a mutual – if twisted – respect and were capable of working together, although their shared love for the *Black Pearl* meant they were often competing to captain it.

With the *Pearl* shrunk down, Barbossa had settled for the *Queen Anne's Revenge* – and had done very well for himself, expanding his command to a

64

fleet of pirate ships that reported in and paid him tribute. Docked in Saint Martin, he and the crew of the *Queen Anne's Revenge* were celebrating a recent "business success".

Two of the men fought over a pair of gold candlesticks. Another drank from a Chinese vase. The rest feasted on rare cuts of meat and guzzled fine imported rum. The ship was littered with life-sized statues, fine paintings, elegant silks, hand-woven rugs, silver and chests of jewels and coins.

Of course, Barbossa, as captain, had first choice of the "inventory". Dressed in a finely embroidered jacket and silk shirt, he rested his solid-gold peg leg on a velvet footstool in his personal quarters. Humming to himself, he carefully recorded the best items from their recent plunders in a ledger, popping some sugary orange candies in his mouth.

Two of his men, Mullroy and Murtogg, burst in, spoiling his mood. They bumbled through an apology for disturbing him, their prattling nearly driving Barbossa mad.

"Speak," he snapped, raising his gun and pointing it at them. "Quickly."

"It's your ships, sir," Murtogg said apologetically.

"Three so far," Mullroy explained. "Attacked by an enemy that takes no riches and kills without provocation. A captain named Salazar left one man on each ship to tell the tale. Soon enough he'll sink your entire fleet."

Barbossa could almost smell the supernatural forces at work. Fortunately, he had a consultant in black magic who happened to currently be imprisoned on the isle of Saint Martin.

* * *

The cell door moaned as it swung open, and Barbossa peered into the shadows. He could just make out the glint of eyes in the darkness. Then Shansa, a beautiful but strange woman, leaned forward to stir a steaming pot bubbling with a sour-smelling liquid. A large rat crawled around her shoulders. Unlike Carina, this woman was a true witch.

"I've been expecting you," said Shansa as she caressed her hissing vermin.

She stared at him, her expression calculating. Barbossa didn't want her to decide on a price for the information he needed.

"Shansa, you and I made our deal long ago,"

he said quickly. "I saved you from the gallows. Remember?"

"And I cursed your enemies," the sea witch said, parrying. "But now you come to me in fear – as the dead have taken command of the sea." She gazed at him a beat longer, then relented, giving him the information he desired. "They are searching for Jack Sparrow. He will sail for the Trident with a girl – and a *Pearl*."

"The Trident will never be found," Barbossa said, scoffing. Jack's quest would be a failure. Barbossa himself had studied the ancient texts and had given up the search long before.

Shansa shrugged, then tossed the rat into the boiling green liquid. Through the steam, Barbossa could see a ship materialize. It was being attacked by the *Silent Mary*.

"The dead are conquering the sea, but they are unable to step on dry land," she cooed. "But nothing else can stop them." When Barbossa curled his lip in disgust at the idea, the witch smirked at him. "Ask yourself this, Captain: is your treasure worth dying for?"

"Aye," he answered. "I'm a pirate. Always will be.

How do I save what be mine?"

Shansa reached into her pocket and produced a familiar object – Jack's compass. One of Barbossa's eyebrows arched in surprise. *How did she get that?* he wondered. But he knew better than to ask her to reveal the secrets of her sorcery.

"It points you to the thing you desire most," said Shansa. She swung the scratched but still shining compass before his fascinated eyes. "But betray that compass and it releases your greatest fear."

"And every pirate's fear," Barbossa said, "is Salazar!"

"Lead them to Jack before he finds the Trident, and all your treasure will come back to you," she said, holding out the compass.

Barbossa grabbed it, knowing it was more precious than all the riches in his cabin. "Time to make a deal with the dead."

CHAPTER SEVEN

THE SUN ROSE OVER THE SLEEPY TOWN OF
Saint Martin as Jack was dragged down the hallway
by guards, happy that this was the day they'd be
rid of his presence. Jack was less enthusiastic about
his impending execution and didn't make their job
easy.

The same crowd who'd come to see the bank
opening had gathered in the square, this time in
their second-best clothes. Executions were more
informal but no less of a community event.

Jack entered the square in a prison carriage,
trapped by bars. He heard the rowdy audience and
spotted several other prisoners, including Carina
and other assorted "witches" in another cage. More
carriages rolled in from the jail, until so many
prisoners had arrived there were more people

awaiting their executions than watching them.

Mayor Dix scurried around, overseeing the proceedings. He nodded at several food and drink vendors as he passed. Each had agreed to raise prices for the event and give the difference to His Honour. The proceeds – some of them, anyway – would help fund construction of a new bank, which the mayor thought only fair, considering Jack had been the one to destroy it. Now the spectacle of his execution would balance the scales.

High up on the church tower, Henry crouched where no one could see him, holding a stout rope. He hoped Carina would be pleased with what he was about to do. Most of all, he hoped it would work.

An enormous guard pulled Jack from his cage. "How would you like to die, pirate?" he asked brightly. "Hanging, firing squad, or a new invention – the guillotine?"

"Guillotine," Jack answered as if choosing a fine wine. "Sounds French. I love the French. They invented mayonnaise. How bad can it be?"

Slapping Jack on the back as though he

approved of the decision, the guard twisted Jack's body in the direction of the new machine.

Jack's eyes widened at the sight. *That's how bad*, he thought. The contraption was as tall as a building. A razor-sharp blade hung in a long frame above two wooden braces. The upper brace had a half circle cut into the bottom edge, the lower one had a half circle in its top edge. Clearly, the victim's head was to be locked in place by the braces – right in the path of the blade above. When a rope was released, the blade flew down and....

"I've changed my mind – like to go with firing squad," Jack said in a rush. "Blindfold!"

Ignoring him, two burly, sweating executioners stepped forward, their heads covered by black masks. One of them placed a large basket next to the guillotine. Jack swallowed hard at the sight of the severed heads inside.

"I'm not one to complain," he said, "but this basket is full of heads. Could I get a fresh one?" He grinned hopefully.

The executioners strapped Jack down to the frame, forcing his head onto the lower half circle and fastening the other plank in place to keep him below the blade. Right in front of his nose sat the basket, ready to catch his head.

"Here's an idea," Jack suggested casually. "Why don't we try a good old-fashioned stoning? Gets the crowd involved, eh?"

The crowd *was* getting impatient, their catcalls rising in volume as they shouted for the show to begin. On a gallows platform across the square from Jack, Carina stood bravely, even when the noose was placed around her neck. There was nothing she could do, but she would die with dignity, and her last words, for anyone who bothered to listen, would be reasonable.

"Good sirs," she began, "I am not a witch. But I forgive your common, dim-witted and feeble brains. In short, most of you have the minds of a goat −"

Jack interrupted, bellowing loudly, "Is it not common practice to be offered a last meal?"

"I believe I was making a point," Carina snapped, irritated by Jack's cavalier attitude. She was not surprised the sneaky, backstabbing pirate had been captured, and she couldn't say she felt bad about his impending fate, although she rather wished it could have been separated from her own. "If you could just be patient."

"My head is about to be lopped off – hence the urgency." Jack raised his hands as far as he could, gesturing at the guillotine.

"And my neck is to be broken."

"On occasion the neck doesn't break. I've seen men swing for hours."

Carina rolled her eyes. "Kill that filthy pirate," she told the executioner. At least she wouldn't have to listen to him prattling on and on. "I'll wait."

"I wouldn't hear of it," said Jack. "Witches first."

"*I am not a witch!*" Carina shouted. "Were you not listening?"

"Sorry, hard to listen with the mind of a goat," Jack quipped.

"*Enough!*" Scarfield commanded. A sense of humour was not his strong point. "Kill them both!"

Jack watched the executioner approach the switch that would release the glinting blade. He closed his eyes.

On cue, Henry heroically swung down from the tower, aiming for the executioner. But he'd miscalculated and flew past the platform, crashing into several soldiers at the centre of the square instead.

Henry leaped to his feet and began to fight his way towards the platform, throwing punches at the soldiers who had him surrounded.

"Get another noose. He will die with the others," said Scarfield from the stands. Sneering down at Henry, he added, "Did you really think you could defeat us, boy?"

"No, sir," said Henry. "I'm just the diversion. *Fire!*"

BOOM!

A cannon blast sounded as Scrum, Gibbs and 10 more from Jack's crew fired into the square.

The explosion caused instant hysteria: soldiers broke formation and civilians stampeded in every direction. The shock of the blast caused the guillotine platform to crack and split apart.

The blade began to fall towards Jack's head. Then it shot back up as the entire guillotine tipped upside down. Jack wound up dangling from the inverted machine of death, the blade shining below him.

"Fire!" Gibbs roared over the chaos.

The second blast sent the crowd, the soldiers and the horses into a total frenzy. Many scrambled in Jack's direction, pushing the guillotine back over. Jack swung helplessly as the whole structure spun – pointing the blade back towards him.

CRASH! Overcome by its own weight and the momentum from the stampeding crowd, the guillotine collapsed, smashing into nothing more than a pile of kindling. But the blade was still in motion. It whisked down to Jack.

With a whack it landed between his legs.

Jack stared at it for a moment, then twisted as his trusty first mate ran forward.

"Gibbs!" Jack cried happily. "I knew you'd come crawling back."

"The Turner boy paid us ten pieces of silver to save your neck," Gibbs replied.

"Very well, I'll pardon your insubordination and grant you absolution," Jack announced. He thought a moment. "You can save me for a small fee. The cost is 10 pieces –"

"That's madness!" said Gibbs. "We won't pay more than five!"

A torrent of gunfire rained down on them. Jack pivoted, using the guillotine board as a shield to block the swords of two soldiers who attacked him.

He ran into the fray, the awkward weight of the guillotine board causing him to fall backwards. Luckily, the board broke as he crashed to the ground, and he was set free.

With a third blast of cannon fire, the British command building crumpled. The crowd, still in hysterics, pushed the soldiers farther and farther back. Jack's crew was fighting well: Gibbs hit one soldier over the head with a piece of the guillotine while Marty's punch sent another man tumbling into the food carts.

"Henry," called Jack to the young man running past him, "find your witch!"

Carina, meanwhile, hadn't been waiting around, but although she'd been struggling to free her hands, they were still bound tight, the noose lying around her pale throat. Henry punched his way through the troops towards her. Only a metre from Carina, Scrum was wrestling with a soldier.

Scrum managed to fling the soldier off his back off the platform.

"Thank you," Carina said to the pirate.

"M'lady." Scrum bowed so deeply, one of his arms hit the switch that activated Carina's gallows.

The floor dropped from under Carina's feet.

Screaming, she fell straight down into the small square hole. When she was at the very point of reaching the limit of the rope around her neck, two strong hands grasped her legs and interrupted her fall.

Carina looked down. It was Henry who clutched her tightly, holding her aloft with the last of his strength.

"From this moment on, we are to be allies," he panted. "We find the Trident together. Do I have your word?"

"You're holding everything but my word," she said. "Now cut me down!"

"I don't have a sword at the moment," Henry said, realizing he really should see about acquiring one of those.

"You came to rescue me without a sword? What kind of soldier are you?"

"Perhaps we could discuss this later?" Henry grunted as he adjusted his grip, trying to boost her higher.

A tall figure approached them in the dim light under the scaffold, the hiss of his voice identifying him as Scarfield.

"Well, look at this," the lieutenant said, drawing his sword. "If I kill the coward, the witch hangs. Two for the price of one."

"Don't let go!" Carina cried.

"It'll be difficult once he kills me," Henry replied, trying to think quickly as Scarfield lunged forward, a nasty grin on his face. Henry braced himself when, suddenly, a sharp thump on the head knocked the lieutenant unconscious. As the officer slumped to the side, Carina and Henry saw Jack standing above them. Scarfield had been subdued by the flat end of the very thing intended to end Jack's life – the guillotine blade.

"Gentlemen," said Jack to the crew behind him, "these two prisoners will lead us to the Trident."

"Prisoners?" Henry objected as he watched the pirates surround them. "I convinced your men to save you – paid them with my own silver. We had a deal!"

"There's been a slight modification," said Jack.

"Six is my final offer!" said Gibbs.

"Done," said Jack, taking the money. "Let's sail!"

CHAPTER EIGHT

IN THE TIME SINCE THE *DYING GULL* HAD LOST its captain and crew, it had listed further on the beach, sinking deeper into the sand.

Nevertheless, Jack Sparrow stepped grandly to the wheel to assume his mighty command. He was a captain once again, even though his ship was immobile – something the crew could remedy shortly, no doubt.

"So this was your plan?" said Carina as she and Henry were tied to the mast. "To be captured and tortured by pirates?"

"You said you needed a ship!" Henry shot back.

"You call this a ship? We're on sand! There's no water!"

Henry shifted uncomfortably, hiding his own doubts. "Jack knows what he's doing."

Meanwhile, the crew had driven thin wooden slats, each roughly half a metre apart from the next, under the hull of the *Dying Gull*. Jack's idea was that once an attached rope was cut, the slats would tumble, allowing the ship to slide into the water. The crew worried it was more likely to slide them into their graves, but Jack was their captain.

"Cut the shard!" Jack bellowed.

The ship lurched, practically throwing itself at the ocean. Then, just as quickly, it stopped short of the water. The crew members jolted forwards, screaming at the tops of their lungs.

There was just one slat left keeping the ship aground. It seemed an eternity before it hit the water. With a resounding boom, the ship glided forward.

"She floats!" cheered Scrum, the rest of the crew celebrating with him. The *Dying Gull* was on its way to the open sea.

Jack knew who was waiting out there: Salazar. Nevertheless, he had his ship, his crew, a little Turner and an impertinent witch who claimed she could understand the Map No Man Can Read. His luck seemed to be slowly returning.

Pike walked up to Jack. "Captain, the British stabbed me with this sword during the battle," he said. "I believe it's yours – a double-edged bone-and-steel cutlass?"

In abject terror, Jack took the cursed sword. Holding it between thumb and forefinger, as if it were covered with worms, he again tossed it into the sea.

* * *

Aboard the *Queen Anne's Revenge*, Barbossa's crew anxiously glanced at their captain. Had he lost his mind? It was madness to head the ship directly into a storm. Even worse, rumours swirled that Barbossa intended to seek out the *Silent Mary*.

But why would their captain steer them to their death?

"Is there a reason, as captain," said Murtogg, ever so carefully, "you've chosen to sail in this unreasonable direction?"

Barbossa merely smiled as he gripped the wheel. "Tell the men we're to be boarded."

As the crew had feared, the *Silent Mary* appeared among the dark clouds ahead. Its battered hull sailed straight for the *Queen Anne's Revenge*. Barbossa studied it, his face a blank mask.

"Sir, turn the wheel!" Mullroy pleaded.

Like a corpse levitating from its tomb, the top of the *Silent Mary* began to rise. The massive hull opened its skeletal jaws ever wider, as though the *Revenge* were about to be eaten. Barbossa didn't flinch.

Staring directly across their ships at Captain Salazar, Barbossa said calmly, "I hear you're looking for Jack Sparrow."

The *Silent Mary* stopped, suspended in the air. Then its crew leaped weightlessly aboard the *Revenge*, their weapons at the ready. Barbossa's crew was frozen in place.

"Hold point and await orders!" Salazar's lieutenant barked at the ghostly army.

Captain Salazar stalked over to Barbossa and planted himself in front of the living man. He noticed Barbossa gazing at the gaping hole in his skull.

"It's impolite to stare," Captain Salazar said. "Have you never seen a fatal wound before?"

"My name is Captain Barbossa, and I stand

before you with cordial intent."

"*'Cordial intent'*?" Captain Salazar repeated. "Do you hear that, men? I am going to show you what 'cordial intent' means. Every time I tap my sword, one of your men will die. So I suggest you speak quickly."

With one tap, a scream of horrendous pain was heard from elsewhere on the ship.

"Tell your men to quiet their screams," Salazar said with a second tap, which prompted another scream. "I have a headache." He tapped again and someone else shrieked. "Tell me where Jack Sparrow is!"

"He's going for the Trident —" Barbossa began.

"There is no treasure that can save him!" bellowed Salazar. "He will *die*! As will *you*!"

Barbossa stood his ground even as Salazar levelled his sword at him. "I be the only one who can lead you to him," Barbossa said firmly. "I declare you'll have Jack's life before sunrise on the morrow – or you can take mine. Do we have an accord?"

Captain Salazar eyed the pirate in disdain. He hated delaying justice for this ship, but if the man could truly take him directly to Jack.... He lowered his sword to his side.

"Take me to him and you will live to tell the tale."

"You have my word," Barbossa said. "I thank you on behalf of my crew."

But Salazar had given no guarantees on that front. With a grim smirk, he tapped five more times. A chorus of screams pierced the air. Barbossa kept his face carefully blank, not wanting to provoke the dead further.

"You can take what's left of them," Salazar said. "The living come aboard!" he ordered his men.

A plank dropped to bridge the two ships. Barbossa, now looking a bit uneasy, followed Salazar onto the *Silent Mary*. What was left of his crew inched their way behind him.

Reaching the deck, Barbossa and his men walked down the line of willowy dead crew. The ghosts, standing to attention, fought their intense urge to kill all the men.

Captain Salazar stretched his arms out wide in a gesture of hospitality. "Welcome to the *Silent Mary!*"

In the shadows of dead seagulls circling above, Barbossa went to the helm and took the wheel.

His downcast crew watched the *Revenge* fade away into the distance as Barbossa sneaked a glance at the compass he had hidden in his pocket. Adjusting the course of the *Silent Mary*, Barbossa hoped the spectral ship was fast. The sooner he could get off it, the better.

CHAPTER NINE

FAR AWAY, JACK SPARROW'S CREW FOUGHT TO keep the *Dying Gull* afloat. Henry and Carina were still tied to the mast, their prospects not looking any brighter.

Jack was up in the crow's nest, scanning the horizon with a spyglass. Henry knew what he was watching for.

"Carina, there's something you need to know," Henry said. "The dead are sailing straight for us."

"Is that so?" Carina asked, her tone disbelieving. "I never should have saved you," she muttered.

Henry gritted his teeth, hoping she didn't mean it. Yes, his plan had gone awry, but at least they were on their way to the Trident.

"Last night there was a blood moon, just as you described. Tell me what it revealed and I promise to help you," he said.

Carina gave him the best cold stare she could muster. "I've been alone my whole life. I don't need any help."

"Then why did you come to me, Carina? Why are we tied together in the middle of the sea, chasing the same treasure? Maybe you can't see it, but our destiny is undeniable."

"I don't believe in destiny," she said. But as he gazed earnestly at her, part of her did want to believe. She shook her head fiercely. Who was he, anyway? An overgrown boy who thought the world was a playground of fanciful creatures and scary ghosts.

Carina had long before learned she couldn't depend on anyone. She had been disappointed too many times. The stars and planets above, though – they went on forever. They would always be there.

"Then believe in me," Henry said softly, "as I believe in you."

Carina stared at him. Why did she so desperately want to trust him? Then again, his words had prompted her to use the ruby as a lens. Maybe he could help her.

"The moon revealed a clue, Henry," she told

him. "'To release the power of the sea, all must divide.'"

"What does it mean?" Henry asked.

"I don't know," Carina said quietly, her voice laced in frustration.

"Then we'll find out," he said confidently. "Together."

Just then Jack appeared before them, holding up the diary.

"There is no map in here," he said, his voice laced with accusation and betrayal.

"Give me that!" cried Carina.

"Give me the Map No Man Can Read," said Jack.

"I can't," she said. "It does not yet exist."

That alarmed several crewmen.

"She's a witch!" cried Marty.

"I'm not a witch," said Carina indignantly. "I'm an astronomer."

"So ... you breed donkeys?" asked Scrum, scratching his head.

"No, I contemplate the sky." Carina had known a lot of ignorant men in her time, but these pirates seemed the worst.

"On a donkey?"

Young Henry Turner swears to free his cursed father, Will, from the *Flying Dutchman*.

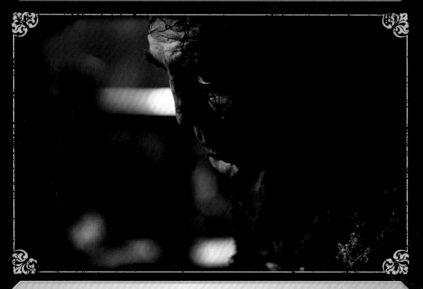

The fearsome Captain Salazar vows to take revenge on Captain Jack Sparrow.

Jack Sparrow finds himself inside the
Royal Bank of Saint Martin.

Jack Sparrow's pirate crew robs the bank –
by stealing the whole building!

An astronomer on a mission, Carina Smyth peers through a telescope at Swift and Sons Chart House.

Carina and Jack are not welcome at the chart house.

Disguised as a nun, Carina asks Henry about his search for the Trident of Poseidon.

Carina makes calculations on the wall of her prison cell.

Captain Hector Barbossa sits in his private quarters on his extravagant ship, the *Queen Anne's Revenge*.

Barbossa seeks help from the witch Shansa to learn more about Salazar's deadly quest for Captain Jack Sparrow.

Henry comes to help save Jack and Carina
from being executed.

Betrayed and taken prisoner by Jack and his crew,
Henry and Carina are tied to the mast of the *Dying Gull*.

The pirates look over Carina's most prized possession –
Galileo's diary.

Before he was cursed, Captain Salazar hunted down
pirates on the *Silent Mary*.

Barbossa and his crew arrive in Hangman's Bay
and halt Jack's unwanted wedding.

Carina guides the *Black Pearl* using the pages
from Galileo's diary.

"There is no donkey!" she burst out.

"She's a *witch*!" The crew drew their weapons.

Jack stepped in front of Carina and pointed his gun at Henry. "Allow me to simplify this equation. Give me the map or I'll kill him."

"Go ahead and kill him," said Carina with a casual air. "You're bluffing."

"And you're blushing." Jack smiled, wagging his finger at her. Then he yelled to the crew: "Throw him over!"

As the men tied a long rope to Henry's hands and dragged him to his feet, Henry looked back at Carina.

"He doesn't appear to be bluffing, Carina!" Those were the only words he managed before they stuffed a gag into his mouth.

"We call this keelhauling," explained Jack, as if he were teaching a class. "Young Henry will be tossed over and dragged under the ship."

Over the side Henry went. Carina stared at Jack, trying her best not to react.

"He just went under the ship," Gibbs narrated from the rail. "If he's lucky, he'll drown before the barnacles slice him to ribbons."

"Barnacles?" Carina's expression faltered.

"Like a thousand knives across your back," said Jack, leaning towards her. "And, of course, the blood attracts sharks."

Carina folded. "We're wasting time! Bring him up!" she cried. She pointed over her head. "The map is there!"

Marty was confused. "The map is ... on your finger?"

"The map is in the *heavens*!" Carina declared impatiently. "The diary will lead me to a map that is written in the stars. Bring him up and I'll find it tonight!"

"Sorry," said Jack slyly as he loosened her bonds. "Can't bring him up. Look for yourself."

Breathless, Carina ran to look over the side. There on the water's surface bobbed a little boat, a gagged Henry safe inside. He had never been in danger at all. He waved to her.

Jack grinned. "Like I said: blushing. I know how this works. The stolen glances, beads of sweat on the brow and behind the neck." He stopped, peering at her. "Have you always been this sweaty?"

"You are confused. I am here for one reason.

He means nothing to me," said Carina, convincing no one. "Now give me the diary and stay out of my way!"

Jack handed her the book. "The scent of desire does not lie," he said. Looking down, he added, "Although that *could* be me."

* * *

The guards leading Shansa, the sea witch, down the dark hall of the jail were heavily armed. Nevertheless, they nervously kept a safe distance from her. Even the prisoners in the cells recoiled as she passed. None of them wanted to fall under an evil spell.

Scarfield stood in the shadows of the jail, waiting for the strange young woman. At the sight of him, Shansa lifted her hands in the air. With a whoosh, all the cell doors flew open at once.

"You dare to try and take me?" she shouted.

Scarfield remained stoic. "A soldier washed ashore talking about the Trident of Poseidon. He was looking for Jack Sparrow – the same pirate who saved a witch from the gallows."

Shansa frowned. "She is no witch."

"But you are," said Scarfield. He motioned to the cell behind him, the wall of which Carina had turned into an astronomy chart. "You're going to read that wall for me … or you will die. I want to know where Jack Sparrow is going with that witch."

Shansa cocked her head, studying him. "I'll set the course for you, but in return, you will set me free."

Scarfield gritted his teeth at the thought of releasing a witch. First things first, he told himself. Let's see what she could tell him.

CHAPTER TEN

NIGHT FELL AND CARINA PACED AT THE *DYING*
Gull's bow, waiting for the lunar eclipse.

Henry watched her, fascinated by the way the
moonlight caressed her features. He realized that if
she knew the amount of years he'd spent studying
the myths and legends she found ridiculous, she'd
be appalled and call it a waste of his time. But as
sharp as her mind was, her life had been sheltered
on land. Henry knew all too well what dangers the
sea held.

When Carina noticed he was staring, he quickly
looked away, which was how he noticed the flashes
of lightning off the starboard side. He hurried to
find Jack.

To his immense frustration, Jack was fast asleep,
a bottle of rum at his side. Henry dashed a bucket

of water on him.

"What are you doing?" Jack spluttered as he sat up. "It's not my week to bathe!"

"Look out to sea," Henry cried. "The dead are hunting us down and you do nothing!"

"Nothing," Jack protested. "You call this nothing?"

"You're drunk and sleeping," Henry scolded him.

"Exactly. I'm doing two things at once."

That did it. Exasperated, Henry lifted a sword from the deck and swung it towards the indifferent pirate. "Like it or not, you're going to help me, Jack. I will break my father's curse!"

"Lighten your grip, square the pommel, front leg bent," Jack instructed, unperturbed by the weapon at his chest. He reached up and adjusted the angle of the sword in Henry's hand. "Much better. Now, run me through."

"What?" Henry felt lost.

"Your first murder!" said Jack. "Happy to be a part of it. Don't mind the blood and screaming – I'll try to keep it down."

Tentatively, Henry pushed the blade against

Jack's skin.

"One quick strike should kill me," Jack advised. "If you'd like, I could get a running start and hop onto the blade."

Henry hesitated. "Maybe I'm not a pirate," he sighed, placing the sword back on the deck where he'd found it. "But you're wrong if you think I wouldn't do it."

Within a breath, Jack had a gun to Henry's head. "And you're wrong if you think I'd ever let you," he growled. "Next time you raise a sword, be the last to die."

Carina walked past, ignoring them completely as she stared at the sky. Jack's gaze drifted from her to Henry.

"In case you were wondering, one holds a woman the same as a sword," he said to the young man. "I suggest you entice her with flattery."

"I'm not interested in Carina!" Henry protested, the flush on his cheeks betraying him.

"I knew it," said Jack with a snort. "She's all you think of! A bit of discretion when courting a redhead – never pursue her sister. But if you cannot avoid the charms of her sister, kill her brother. And if she gives you a piece of salted meat, assume it's poisoned – unless she's a twin, in which case, still kill her brother. Savvy?"

"I do *not* savvy!" said Henry. Why was Jack talking about redheads? Carina's hair was a beautiful layered brown, like coffee beans scattered over a cedar floor. Perhaps, Henry conceded to himself, he'd been thinking of her a little.

Jack held out his palm. "That wisdom will cost you five pieces."

* * *

Scarfield's soldiers surrounded Shansa as she positioned herself at the back wall of the cell that had recently held Carina. They didn't understand the meaning of the strange stars and lines Carina had drawn there. Scarfield was certain the witch could read them, though.

Slowly, Shansa stretched her hand up as far as it could go. At her touch, a single drop of blood oozed from the solid surface. The men drew back, aghast, as the drop grew into a line. Soon there were several bloody lines running across the wall.

The lines started to run together, tracing a

shape. Soon the image of a Trident was clearly visible, etched in deep red.

"A soldier will hold the power of the sea – a weapon like none before," Shansa intoned. "The Trident will be found."

"A soldier?" said Scarfield, his chest tightening at the thought of owning such power.

Shansa smirked. She did not need magic to know what he was dreaming of; the fool was as transparent as glass to her.

"Ask yourself, Lieutenant: is this a treasure worth dying for?" She raised an eyebrow in challenge, already knowing what his response would be.

Scarfield took a low, deep breath and clenched his fists. "Ready the *Essex*," he ordered the soldiers. "We will sail immediately!"

* * *

Henry was peering through his spyglass when Carina appeared next to him on the deck of the *Dying Gull*.

"What are you doing?" she asked.

"Looking for my father," replied Henry. "Even when I know he's not there."

"Just because you can't see something doesn't mean it's not there," Carina reminded him. "Like the map."

Henry lowered the spyglass and turned to her, his face serious. "No one has ever found it. Maybe it doesn't exist."

"Doesn't exist?" Carina's voice was sharp. "This diary is the only truth I know. I kept it with me each day in the orphanage – studied the heavens when it was forbidden, when they called me a witch and wanted to hang me! I swore to know the sky as my father intended me to!"

Henry pondered how similar his past was to Carina's; both had grown up without their fathers but were nevertheless guided by them, like a needle on a compass. He knew she would not rest until she felt she'd honoured her father's wishes, just as Henry could not give up on his quest to free his father.

"Carina," he said gently, "you're always looking to the sky. Perhaps the answer is right here." He gestured to the diary.

Carina flipped through it. Maybe there was something she had overlooked. She showed Henry a note from Galileo she'd found inside – which she had translated into English: "All truths will be understood once the stars align."

But stars cannot move, much less align, she thought. He could have meant planets, but then why were stars in the drawing?

Henry peered over her shoulder, his finger hovering above the words. Then an idea occurred to him.

"Carina," he said, "Galileo was Italian. But *'directus'* is not Italian, it's Latin. *'Directus'* means 'straight line' in Latin."

"'All truths will be understood'," Carina said, working it out, "'once the stars are in a *straight line!'* It was right in front of me! There is a straight line moving from Orion – the son of Poseidon."

"But how do you follow it?" Henry asked.

With renewed excitement, Carina pulled the ruby from the book. Using it as a lens, she held it aloft instead of over the book. She and Henry both looked through to see the answer: a red line running across the sky, intersected by another.

It was the Map No Man Can Read!

"A straight line starting in Orion – the hunter's

arrow moving straight through Cassiopeia – heading across the sky towards the end of the Southern Cross. It ends there – Henry!"

"So the map is inside the cross?" Henry asked.

"No, the Southern Cross is an X hidden in the sky since the beginning of time!" Carina explained.

"It will lead us to the Trident! We just have to follow the X!" Henry exclaimed.

Click. Behind them they heard a pistol being cocked.

"And X always marks the spot," Jack observed with a wry smile.

CHAPTER ELEVEN

CAPTAIN SALAZAR CROSSED THE DECK OF THE *Silent Mary* to confront Barbossa at the wheel.

"The Sun is up – and so is your time," Salazar growled.

Barbossa glanced down at Jack's compass, still concealed in his coat, then up to the horizon.

"Not to disagree, but our accord ends at Sunrise," he said to the ghostly captain. "This be but first light – far from a fully risin' Sun. And you being a man of honour –"

"Silence!" Salazar cried. "You know nothing of me!"

But Barbossa did know – at least, he had heard the stories. They told of a mighty Spanish captain named El Matador del Mar who scoured the ocean of ships. No one else attacked with such ferocity.

"I know you've hunted and killed thousands of men," Barbossa said of the carnage.

"Men?" said Salazar. "No, no, not men. Pirates."

Captain Salazar decided to set the record straight; if Barbossa fulfilled his end of the agreement, Salazar would leave him alive to spread the tale.

"Years ago I swore to rid the seas of every pirate who sailed – and that is what I did. I destroyed dozens of ships until there were only a handful left. The last ones joined together to try to defeat me. But they soon realized it was hopeless. Nothing could stop my *Silent Mary*." Salazar's voice rang with pride. "Their ships went down one by one."

As Salazar spoke, the image of a very different *Silent Mary* crystallized in Barbossa's mind. Such a fine figure of a ship it was, too...

Four wooden gun towers lined the perimeter of the Silent Mary. *They loomed several metres over the deck, and from the openings at the top, soldiers manned a full arsenal of cannons and guns that could be directed at enemy ships.*

A striking, darkly handsome young man walked the deck, surveying his crew as they lined up their guns. It was the trim, athletic Captain Salazar. He lifted his head to the Sun, sure the clear day was a blessing on him for the ensuing battle with the pirates. The weather was mild. The waters had just a light chop. There were no hazards for miles and nowhere for the pirates to hide. The only thing on the horizon was a minor rock formation. Salazar ordered full speed ahead.

The Silent Mary cut gracefully through the water as it drew abreast of one of the pirate ships. The smaller vessel didn't stand a chance.

Salazar smiled as his men fired the cannons. The pirate ship crumbled, its planks splintered into pieces by the Silent Mary's guns, a Jolly Roger flag caught in the debris.

Salazar's first mate, Lieutenant Lesaro, came up next to him and they both gazed at the waves below, where several of the pirates clung to driftwood, their free hands signalling the Silent Mary in desperation.

"Those men in the water are surrendering, sir," Lieutenant Lesaro said. "Begging for mercy." The lieutenant's eyes softened as he considered the pitiful figures below, but his captain's stern voice brought him back to attention.

"Mercy?" Captain Salazar spat. "You wish to give them mercy?" He turned his head, ice coating his gaze as it pinned Lesaro to the spot. The lieutenant may be weakening, but Salazar would infuse him with his own strength of will.

"You know my father was an admiral. And a traitor," Salazar said, his tone flat. "He patrolled these very waters. But he took bribes from pirates – gold and silver – and allowed them to sail with impunity!" The captain's lip curled in disgust. "He was arrested when I was a boy and soon after, they came to our house and took my mother away – dragged her to a workhouse. The wife of a traitor must pay for his sins."

Lesaro was unnerved to see Salazar's face take on an unusually pained expression. His captain had never shown any vulnerability before. Yet a heartbeat later, the captain's features hardened. He plucked a knife from his belt and turned it over and over in his hands.

"A year after she died in there, my father was released from prison. When he returned home, I greeted him with this knife, gutted him like the coward he was," he said. "And that day I made a vow to myself. I would kill them all."

Plunging his knife into the rail, Salazar glared at the pirates thrashing in the water. Their desperate movements made them look like the rats they were.

"There will be no mercy," he pronounced.

Upon their captain's nod, the crew fired a volley into the sea. As the smoke cleared, a few survivors could be seen swimming away.

"Fire!" Lesaro shouted. He was a loyal soldier and would follow his captain anywhere. The men leaped to obey, re-loading cannons and guns along the deck.

As the last of the pirate ships burned, Salazar smiled and turned back to Lesaro.

"The waters are finally pure. Their wretched flags will no longer stain the sea," he said. His heart felt at peace. He'd achieved his goal.

Or so he thought.

On a nearby pirate ship, the crew worked to smother the flames as another blast rocked the deck. The captain staggered and collapsed at the feet of a black-haired teen, the youngest pirate aboard.

"Captain!" The pirate called in alarm. He dropped to his knees and reached out, as if he could stem the flow of blood from the captain's wounds with his bare hands.

The grizzled pirate reached into his breast pocket and pulled out a golden compass. Pressing it into the young man's hands, he whispered urgently.

"It's up to you now, Jack. This compass will point to

what you want most. Don't betray it. The pirate's life must live on."

Jack nodded fiercely, his eyes bright, but when he stood, he found the crew looking to him now for leadership. Taking a deep breath, he flipped open the compass and looked down. Without hesitation, the needle snapped to a stop, pointing the way.

Swiftly, Jack set the course and then climbed to the crow's nest to have the best vantage point. As his ship drew abreast of the Silent Mary, the architect of the demise of so many fellow pirates, including his captain, Jack felt a surge of anger followed by a bolt of rebellious bravery. He would outwit Salazar and end the Silent Mary's destructive reign.

"Lovely day for a sail, Captain, wouldn't you agree?" Jack called out jauntily, waving to Salazar.

Salazar turned in amazement. One ship remained and was trying to escape, yet the foolhardy pirate in the crow's nest had the audacity to taunt him. Salazar could barely make out the lad. He was so tiny that he couldn't be seen; from the deck, it looked as if a small bird was perched up there – a sparrow.

"The way I see it," shouted the pirate who would thenceforth be known as Jack Sparrow, "there's just the two of us left. Surrender to me now, Captain, and I will let you live."

Not believing his ears, Salazar raised his spyglass. His eyes blazed in fury as the young man hoisted a pirate flag high, waving it at the Spanish commander. How dare this imp mock him? He would chase him down and run his knife over the upstart's neck himself. When Salazar was finished, the pirate's life would be no more.

The pirate ship darted in the direction of the rock formation. Salazar was unconcerned. There was nowhere to land on that arch. It meant nothing. The capture was everything.

"Follow him in," Salazar ordered.

Aboard the Wicked Wench, Jack swung to the deck and raced towards his men as they stared at the arched entrance into the unknown. They knew nobody who passed into the Devil's Triangle returned.

"Grab some lines, mates!" Jack shouted, breaking into the men's fear. He hauled on a length of rope himself and ran to the rail. "Prepare the bootleg! Port side, throw it now!"

As the pirate ship was about to pass through the gateway, several pirates rushed across the deck as if the devil himself were chasing them to join Jack. Together they hurled the ropes towards the rocks.

Jack was either brilliant or just lucky – because the ropes snapped around the boulders at the entrance. The pirate at the wheel turned it farther, and as the ropes pulled tight, the ship rotated.

To Salazar's shock, the pirate ship made a perfect 180-degree turn. Now it was sailing away from the rock formation. Frantically, Salazar grabbed the wheel and turned with all his might to do the same.

But without the aid of a counterweight such as the one Jack had engineered, it was hopeless. The Silent Mary's great speed carried it under the archway, slamming it into a cluster of rocks. The impact tore a gaping hole in its hull, and one fire after another burst and blazed along the deck.

His ship burning, Captain Salazar stared back through the gateway at the pirate ship that had escaped him with the wretched Jack Sparrow aboard. As the flames licked the barrels of gunpowder evenly spaced along the Silent Mary, there came an explosion so hot and intense it brought the surrounding ocean surface to a boil.

The crew were blown to bits, and the ship crumbled and sank like a delicate dying rose.

Then something very strange happened. As the ship plummeted through the water, Captain Salazar's eyes opened. An unearthly transformation had taken place. He vowed silently that on the day they escaped their prison, Jack Sparrow would pay for his sins.

Above the surf, Jack watched the last of the Silent Mary *succumb to the flames. One by one, the pirates lined up in front of Jack.*

The men reached into their pockets, producing treasured objects and placing them in front of the young man.

"What is this?" Jack asked, confused.

"Tribute," said one of them, "sir."

Jack picked up the items one at a time: a rabbit's foot, an earring, some beads and a red scarf. He held the scarf up to his temple. Just my colour, he thought.

The Sun was setting over the pirate ship. Young Jack Sparrow was now adorned with the spoils of his first success. There was one thing he did not wear, however. Cradled in his hand was a compass of immeasurable power.

"The thing I want most," Jack said softly. Slowly, he lifted the compass. "The pirate's life," he wished.

The needle turned, pointing to the horizon.

CHAPTER TWELVE

MORNING HAD BROKEN OVER THE DECREPIT *Silent Mary*. Barbossa stood, nervously eyeing the bloodthirsty Salazar. He'd have to hope the ghost's personal vendetta against Sparrow would spare Barbossa from the captain's more general hatred of pirates.

"The Sparrow took everything from me," the disfigured Salazar growled. "Left me to rot in the filth of death. Which is where the tale ends for you!"

A trickle of blood seeped from Barbossa's throat as Salazar pressed his blade against it.

"Not yet, Captain!" said Barbossa, motioning towards the horizon. "I found him, as promised."

The *Dying Gull* was visible in the distance. At last, the prize was within Salazar's grasp.

"Jack the Sparrow!" Salazar's face looked nearly

alive again as a manic desire for vengeance passed over his features.

* * *

Jack and his crew squinted at the sky over the *Dying Gull*. None of this map business made sense. It was still the Map No Man Can Read, even if they knew where it was.

"Jack, how are we to follow an X to a spot where no land could exist? An X that has disappeared with the Sun!" Gibbs shook his head as he spoke, completely befuddled by the situation.

"This may very well be the worst map I've ever seen – mainly because I can't see it," said Jack. Leaning towards Carina, he added, "For the last time, how do we find your X?"

Carina flinched away from his breath but otherwise remained cool. "The chronometer keeps the exact time in London," she explained as Jack pretended to follow. "I'm making an altitude measurement to the Southern Cross to determine longitude. Only then will we find that spot on the sea."

When several of the pirates looked dubious,

Carina rolled her eyes, sick of defending herself. "My calculations are precise and true," she said firmly.

"So nobody can find that X but you?" Jack asked. He'd seen stranger things for sure, but it was still odd to him that this girl could navigate with a map nobody else could see. It was no wonder everyone thought she was a witch.

"*Salazar!*" Henry cried as he spotted the deadly ghost ship to their aft.

They all turned to see the *Silent Mary* sailing behind them and closing fast.

"Jack," said Henry urgently, "the dead will not rest until they have their revenge!"

Jack was getting tired of Henry's reminding him of that. In a way, Jack felt it might be a bit of a relief for the dead to go ahead and come, just to shut Henry up. His crew felt otherwise.

"The dead were not part of this deal!" Gibbs exclaimed.

The men began shouting, upset that they had been led to the slaughter. That was the thanks they got for returning to Jack. He brought them more bad luck and a witch besides. They were at the end of their tether.

"We've been fooled for the last time," Scrum cried.

"Kill them all!" shouted Bollard as the entire *Dying Gull* crew drew their weapons on Jack, Carina and Henry.

Jack raised a finger. "Kill me and the dead won't have their revenge," he reminded them.

"Which will anger them even more," added Henry.

"Are all pirates this stupid?" Carina asked no one in particular.

Confused, the crew fell as deep in thought as possible. Some of them scratched their heads with their weapons.

"Jack," Gibbs asked his prisoner, "what should we do?"

"As captain," Jack replied, "might I suggest a mutiny?"

* * *

Thirty minutes later, Jack and Henry hurriedly rowed a longboat towards a small island while the *Dying Gull* made haste in the opposite direction. The *Silent Mary*, for its part, had turned to follow the longboat.

Carina, in the centre of the longboat, felt none of the other two occupants' apprehension. "Mutiny?" she asked Jack. "You had to suggest a mutiny?"

"Carina," Henry panted between strokes. "They're coming."

"Ghosts?" she said, laughing. "You're afraid of ghosts?"

"Yes," Jack answered truthfully. "And lizards. And Quakers."

"Do you not see what's behind us?" Henry asked, amazed that someone so smart could be so thickheaded.

Carina scoffed and looked back. "I see a very old ship," she sniffed, burying a twinge of unease at the sight of the dark clouds surrounding the pursuing vessel. "Nothing more."

As she watched the ship, sails seemed to appear from nowhere, giving their pursuers more speed. They were only a kilometre away, but the rowing boat was a mere hundred metres from the island now.

Coming to a decision, Carina stood up and began to unbutton her dress.

"What are you doing?" Henry asked in alarm.

"Whoever these men are, they're after Jack. And Jack is on this boat! So I'm going to swim for it," Carina explained. It made perfect sense to her.

"How dare you do exactly what I would do if I were you?" asked Jack haughtily, secretly impressed.

"Carina, stop that!" Henry protested as she continued to unfasten her garment. He could feel his cheeks flushing.

"I can't very well swim in this dress," Carina said in exasperation. Undoing the last button, Carina slid out of her dress, yet even without it, her long, elaborate undergarments made her seem nearly just as fully clothed as before.

"This is by far the best mutiny I've ever had," Jack observed.

Ignoring the men, Carina dived into the water and began swimming for the island.

"Jack," said Henry, dazed, "it's not right. I saw her ankles. Both of them."

* * *

Salazar's men descended into the hull of the *Silent Mary*, where a school of sharks they'd killed were hanging. The crew brought the gutted corpses up topside and then threw them into the water. Once the sharks touched the sea, their eyes flew open. They had become rotting ghosts – and faster, more effective killers.

Unaware of the dead sharks darting towards them in the water, Henry stood up in the boat and took off his jacket.

"I'm going after her," he said, preparing to dive in.

"You would leave me after all I've done for you?" Jack asked dramatically. "Pursue some girl in her knickers? We had a deal."

"There's been a slight modification," Henry replied, enjoying the opportunity to throw Jack's words back at him. He moved to the bow of the boat, about to leap overboard.

Needle-sharp jaws snapped only inches from Henry as a reanimated shark lunged up from the water.

"Shark!" Henry yelped, toppling over backwards into the rowing boat.

Several others quickly closed in on the boat, chomping huge bites out of the wood. Henry shouted in alarm and tried to fend them off with an oar while Jack fired at them, but since they were already dead, the sharks were undeterred. The small boat was getting smaller very quickly.

As if the sharks weren't enough to contend with, Henry and Jack saw Salazar's men jump off the *Silent Mary* and land on the water without so much as a splash. Instead of sinking below, they ran across the surface towards the longboat, their swords drawn.

"We have to swim for it," Henry cried. Struck by an idea, he grabbed Carina's dress and began stuffing an oar inside it. "I'll distract them."

"Perfect," Jack drawled. "I'll swim to shore while they eat you!"

Ignoring Jack, Henry finished wrestling the dress on to the oar, then he tossed it as far as he could behind them. As the frilly object splashed down, the sharks darted towards it. Henry wasted no time diving in the opposite direction and headed for shore.

But the sharks had weakened the boat so much Jack's foot broke through the bottom before he could jump. Having torn the decoy dress to shreds, the sharks circled back and spotted Jack's dangling foot. With a tremendous wrench, Jack tried to free his foot from the boat's base; then he noticed a grappling hook at the bottom of the boat.

Just as a massive shark rose from the water and extended its cavernous mouth, Jack lifted the grappling hook high and jammed it into its open jaws. With the rope attached, the shark started pulling the boat.

Jack held tightly to the rope, the boat skimming the water. As he passed Henry, Jack leaned down and dragged him aboard by his collar.

Carina arrived on shore, unaware that not far behind, Jack was steering a dead shark to keep a wrecked boat out of reach of dead pirates.

The ghosts were closing in until Jack yanked on the hook, turning the shark sharply. With a loud crash, the boat cut into the shore, sending sand flying all over Carina.

"What is wrong with you both?" she cried with great annoyance as she wiped her eyes. "Let me guess. You've seen another −"

And there they were − a whole ghastly, ghostly horde hovering at the edge of the water. Nothing had prepared her for such a bone-chilling sight. Unable to move any farther from the water, they stared hungrily at Carina, Henry and, most of all, Jack.

Captain Salazar glared at his prey, only a few inches away. "Jack the Sparrow," he rumbled.

The border between sea and land was like a supernatural fence. Despite this, several ghost soldiers tried to rush forward to grab Jack. They disintegrated in a small explosion, suffering a second grisly demise, this time without coming back.

"They can't step on land!" cheered Jack. "And to think I was worried!"

Carina, who had been struck silent with shock, started stepping back, her mouth wide open. When she could finally speak, there was only one thing to say: *"Ghosts!"*

CHAPTER THIRTEEN

CAPTAIN SALAZAR STOOD FIRM AT THE shoreline, the waves lapping around his feet. Jack was so close he could almost taste his revenge. Salazar had waited that long, though; he could wait a bit longer.

"Do you remember me, Jack?" said Salazar.

"You look the same," Jack replied, eyeing the captain up and down. "Other than that gaping hole in your skull. Are those new boots?"

"You'll soon pay the devil his due," Salazar hissed.

"Ghosts!" Carina yelled again, turning and bolting inland.

Henry called to her, but she disappeared into the trees. With a glance at Jack and the legion of dead lurking at the shore, he raced after her.

"Love to stay and chat," said Jack politely to Salazar, "but my map just ran away!"

Captain Salazar glared at him as he disappeared into the trees. "I'll be waiting for you, Jack," he vowed. "You will know my pain."

Carina didn't know where she was running, only that it had to be as far away as possible from the ghosts. Almost immediately, she ran into a snag in the form of a net, which scooped her up, trapping her in the air. *Filthy pirates*, she thought.

* * *

Back on the *Dying Gull*, Gibbs was relieved that the ghosts had ignored him and the remnants of Jack's crew. The British navy, however, was right on their tail, Scarfield's ship, the *Essex*, bearing down on them.

Gibbs figured that if the navy was going to hold anyone responsible for their pirate escapades, it wasn't going to be him. He rushed to Scrum, the captain's hat in hand.

"Scrum! Good news!" he said. "Jack always told me that if something happened to him, you should be made captain. Now go and take the wheel, son –

and wear the hat of a captain."

Scrum was both delighted and clueless as he carefully placed the hat on his head. "This be my proudest moment indeed."

A half hour later, Captain Scrum found himself taking a brutal beating aboard the *Essex*. Scarfield was using him to set an example for the rest of the pirates – no criminal would escape the might of the British Empire.

"Take them below," Scarfield said, once he felt the pirates were sufficiently cowed.

Gibbs and the men followed behind as the two soldiers dragged a nearly unconscious Scrum to the cells beneath the deck.

Turning back to the ocean, Scarfield adjusted the course based on what the sea witch had told him. No pirates would stand in his way as he sailed for the Trident.

* * *

Jack and Henry had not found a trace of Carina. They walked down the long, hot road leading to the island town of Hangman's Bay. Passing townsfolk eyed them with suspicion.

"I know what's ailing you," said Jack, in a brotherly mood. "I've seen it before in sad, half-witted, idiotic dum-dums like yourself, who so stupidly find themselves out at sea, having left a beautiful, alluring young woman behind, only to have her wind up in the arms of some strapping young bloke with perfect teeth, et cetera, et cetera.... You've got the unscratchable itch!"

"I am not in love with her!" Henry insisted. "She is the only one who can find the Trident!"

That moment, the very person they were speaking of called out, "Help me!" Her cries came from a grove of trees.

Henry and Jack dashed towards her voice and found her suspended in a net. As they got a few steps closer, Jack motioned to Henry and said, "Help her!"

But that was impossible, as another net picked up Jack and Henry, their bodies tumbling together, with Henry's weight pushing Jack against the side. Jack peered out between the cords as a man strode up to them. He looked familiar.

Unfortunately for Jack, the man was part of Pierre "Pig" Kelly's small band of pirates. Like almost everyone in the Caribbean, Pig had a score to settle with Jack. The man was soon joined by his cohorts, who not-so-gently lowered Jack, Henry and Carina to the ground and marched them into town, where Pig and the rest of his crew were waiting for them.

"Pig Kelly," said Jack jovially, "my old friend."

"*Friend?*" Pig laughed. He raised his gun to Jack's head. "You hear that, boys? This lying pirate owes me a plunder of silver. But luck has brought him to Hangman's Bay – and he'll settle his debt right now."

"Of course, Pig," Jack returned. "I've looked everywhere for you, prayed for your safety after inadvertently paying those men to put you in a sack! Name your price."

A strange woman sidled up to Jack and looked him over. She was plump with a scabbed face, rotting yellow teeth and a crooked smile. Jack looked at Carina, standing next to Henry. Someone had put a tattered red dress on her, and there were dead flowers in her hair.

The strange woman was also holding dead flowers. *What is going on?* Jack wondered. *Is it some kind of funeral? Is it* my *funeral?*

Pig introduced the woman as Beatrice. "She's my poor widowed sister," he explained. "She's been looking for a respectable man. But they don't come to this horrid place, so you'll do. This is how you'll clear your debt."

It is *my funeral,* thought Jack. He realized in horror that they were standing in a chapel made from the skeleton of a beached whale. An old gentleman played a wedding march on a broken fiddle.

Beatrice gave Jack her best toothy smile. If only the daisies in the bouquet were as yellow....

"We'll honeymoon in the barn!" she told him.

Jack screamed and tried to run, but a rope had been tied to his neck, the other end attached to the altar like a literal embodiment of the bonds of holy matrimony they were about to force upon him.

A nervous old priest ambled up to the altar.

Pig called out, "Bring the best man and the bridesmaid!" Henry and Carina were shoved into the wedding party. "Pretty girl, Jack," said Pig. "No wonder you were chasing after her. She'll die by your side if you fail to say 'I do'."

125

Two grimy-looking children scampered up to the altar. "Our children," said Beatrice. "Best not to look them in the eye."

Jack's eyes widened in fright. "I looked at the small one!" he gasped.

The priest began the ceremony, then paused for the groom's vows. When Jack refused to say "I do", Pig waved his gun threateningly at the pirate and his companions. Henry and Carina begged Jack to just say the words, but Jack couldn't get them out.

"Last chance," Pig growled, his gun at Carina's temple.

"Wait! This is not legal!" Henry called, his eyes cutting to Carina, who figured out his idea.

"He's right," Carina piped up. "Does any man here object to these nuptials?"

"*I do!*" Jack exclaimed.

"Congratulations!" announced the priest. "You may kiss the –"

Boom!

The wedded "bliss" was cut short by a blunderbuss shot, which blew apart several ribs of the whale carcass. Barbossa stood in the aisle of the chapel, his crew at his back.

"Ah, Jack!" Barbossa said. "We meet again!"

Jack shook his head in surprise. "Hector? Who invited you to my wedding? Did you bring me a present?"

With another quick shot from Barbossa, Pig crumpled to the ground, clutching his leg. The bride and the rest of Pig's crew scattered for the trees. The most beautiful day of Jack and Beatrice's life together was over as quickly as it had begun.

"Thanks," said a giddy Jack to Barbossa. "It's just what I've always wanted. I've missed you so much!"

Barbossa gave him a boyish grin. "I know!"

CHAPTER FOURTEEN

AS HEARTFELT AS THE REUNION BETWEEN JACK and Barbossa seemed, Barbossa's crew was more concerned about the job they'd been sent to do. There was a vengeful ghost who could and would hunt them down waiting for them to bring back a certain prisoner.

"Um, Captain," Mullroy said, "shouldn't we be getting back to Salazar, so we can trade Jack's life for our own?"

Jack felt it was a rather insensitive thing to say, since he was standing right there. How could Mullroy suggest such a thing? Didn't he know it was Jack's wedding day?

"Aye, that we could," Barbossa replied calmly. "But *I* have come for the Trident of Poseidon. And with it, I will gut the dead who stole my command of the sea!"

Murtogg was aghast. "You're going to double-cross the dead?"

"As much as I love this plan," said Jack, "there are two small problems. Firstly, I don't wish to die – and secondly, no vessel can outrun that shipwreck...."

"But there is *one*, Jack," Barbossa assured him, drawing his sword, "and she be the fastest ship at sea – the *Black Pearl* – entrapped in that bottle by Blackbeard five winters ago."

Tink, tink. Barbossa tapped the bottle hidden under Jack's coat. Then he waved his sword dramatically over his head in circles.

"By the power of that blackguard's sovereign blade, I hereby release the *Black Pearl* to claim her former glory!"

Without hesitating, he ran his sword straight towards Jack's heart. *Thunk!* The blade stopped when it hit the glass. Jack's pocket began to vibrate. A tiny crack formed in the bottle, leaking a few drops of water onto Jack's shirt – like a pool of blood.

Realizing what would happen next, Jack sprinted towards the beach, everyone else following close behind. The bottle continued to crack as Jack ran wildly across the sand. With a loud burst, the glass shattered. The *Black Pearl*, at least a small version of it, dropped at Jack's feet.

The ship was no larger than a collector's model, but it quaked in the sand and began to grow. Longer and higher it expanded. When it was the size of a large halibut, it stopped.

Barbossa gave the little ship a good look. It reminded him of a dying fish gasping for air. "She needs the sea," he said with complete certainty.

He picked up the ship and flung it into the ocean, where it made a slight splash. Only instead of floating, the *Pearl* sank quickly beneath the surface, dark waves swallowing it whole.

The pirate captains sadly stared out over the sea. Both of them had loved that ship. There was a gentle frothing on the surface. Then the surrounding surf began to simmer and bubble like the contents of a bean pot.

With a monstrous *ka-fwoosh* the *Black Pearl* rushed from the surface. Rising like a phoenix, it cast a massive shadow along the beach. Sheets of water cascaded off its hull.

Now that the ship was restored, Barbossa had one last detail to clear up. He promptly put a gun to Jack's head.

"There be room for only *one* captain, Jack. Time to race the dead!" Barbossa said.

The crafty pirate laughed as an all-too-familiar little monkey dropped onto his shoulder, finally free from its shrunken prison. The little beast, also named Jack, bared his teeth and let out a searing howl right in Jack's face.

"Monkey breath," said Jack. "I hate that."

* * *

Captain Salazar was getting restless. Barbossa was taking far too long and there was no movement on the beach. Salazar couldn't ignore the feeling that it had been a mistake to trust him, but what choice had there been with Jack on land? There was no way off that island for them in any case; none of the ships he'd seen in the port could match the *Silent Mary*. Still, what could be causing the delay? Extending his spyglass, Salazar turned and scanned the far horizon.

Rage boiled up in his hollow chest. There it was

– none other than the blasted *Black Pearl* itself – racing away from the island at top speed. Barbossa had betrayed him!

"Pirates!" he shrieked.

* * *

The *Black Pearl* was as strong and fast as the day it had first sailed. The crew, feeling as if the good old days had returned, picked up their duties with enthusiasm. Several enjoyed the opportunity to tie Jack to the centre mast as Henry and Carina were bound to the back mast. Barbossa smiled broadly as he steered the *Pearl*, feeling he was back where he belonged. An impertinent voice interrupted his triumphant moment.

"The course you sail must be exact, Captain," Carina said.

"There is no *exact* at sea!" Barbossa growled.

"She's the only one who can follow that X," Henry added.

"Is that a fact?" Barbossa turned to sneer at them. "This girl knows more of the sea than I?"

"You'll follow the Southern Cross to a single reflection point. I have a chronometer which determines longitude. It will take us to an exact spot at sea." Carina stared him down, her blue eyes fierce.

Barbossa's instincts told him she might be right. Scallywag that he was, Barbossa also had more common sense than he had ego.

"Untie them," he ordered. "Take the wheel, miss," he told Carina.

Carina was a little surprised that the pirate captain was willing not only to listen to her but to let her guide the ship. This rogue was actually more open-minded than all of Saint Martin's populace put together.

Henry and Carina felt the eyes of the entire crew on them as they stepped up to the wheel. Carina paused.

"What are you looking at?" she said to the flabbergasted men. "Full to starboard, you indolent scallywags!"

Beside her, Henry smiled, but he noticed Carina's pensive face as the men scurried to obey her orders.

"This ship, those ghosts ... there can be no logical explanation," Carina said softly when Henry gave her an inquisitive look.

"The myths of the sea are real, Carina, as real as my father," Henry said. "I'm glad you can see you were wrong."

"Wrong?" Carina raised her eyebrows. "Perhaps I had some doubts – thought you were mad. One could say I was possibly, arguably a bit –"

"Wrong," Henry supplied. "The word is *wrong*."

"Slightly in error," Carina said, teasing.

Henry shook his head, the corners of his mouth twitching in amusement. "This is the worst apology I've ever heard."

"Why would I apologize?"

"Because we've been chased by the dead and sail on a ship raised from a bottle," Henry replied. "Where is your science in that?"

"It was science that found that map," Carina retorted.

"No," Henry insisted. "We found it together."

"Fine. Then I will apologize. Although, one could argue that you owe me an apology, as my life has been threatened by pirates and dead men."

"Which you now believe in, I'm sorry to say!" Henry said.

"Apology accepted." Carina nodded.

Henry knew when he was beaten. "I'm going to the lookout."

Carina watched him go, now grinning. She quite enjoyed her banter with Henry. But there were more pressing matters at hand: she had an island to find.

* * *

Far into the night, the *Essex* sailed on, using the heading Shansa had given Scarfield. Jack's crew, still imprisoned down below, were looking for something sharp to attempt a breakout. The only thing that might work was a toe bone. Since Scrum was the new captain, they elected his toe for cutting.

"I don't want to be captain anymore," said Scrum as the pirates held him upside down.

Luckily for Scrum, there was a commotion up above and as one of the soldiers rushed by he dropped the keys to the cell. The pirates froze for a beat, waiting for the man to return, then bolted to the bars and scrabbled to reach the keys.

Scarfield had heard the shouts of alarm as well and strode on deck to investigate.

"Ship off the port!" one of his men called.

Through his spyglass, Scarfield saw the *Black Pearl* far in front of the *Essex*. A rowing boat with the unmistakable figure of the sea witch and a cowering group of pirates was halfway between them.

"Prepare the guns!" he shouted. "Those pirates are going for the Trident!"

CHAPTER FIFTEEN

STRONG WINDS HOWLED AROUND CARINA, whipping pieces of her hair into her face, and the waters beneath the *Black Pearl* grew rough, but she stood firm at the helm. Coming to check on their progress, Barbossa noticed the diary in her hand. His eyes narrowed, his heart jolting at the sight.

"Where did you get this, missy?" he said, his speech brusque. "This book be pirate treasure – stolen from an Italian ship many years ago. There was a ruby on the cover I would not soon forget."

"Stolen? You're mistaken." Carina's chin lifted at the accusation, although part of her wondered how he'd known about the gem. She took the ruby from her pocket. "This was given to me by my father, who was clearly a man of science," she said to the pirate. Her eyes sparked angrily as she defended her father. "This diary is my birthright – left with me on the steps of a children's home, along with a name. Nothing more."

"Oh, so you're an orphan?" Barbossa asked, one eyebrow raised. "And what be you called?"

"The brightest star in the north gave me my name," she replied.

Barbossa looked at the young woman as if noticing her for the first time. "Carina."

"Carina Smyth," she said, surprised. "So you know the stars?"

"I'm a captain," he answered softly. "I know which stars to follow home."

As he left, his face was ashen, as though he had seen a ghost. He took Jack's compass out of his pocket. The needle slowly pointed at Carina.

The captain backed away until he bumped into Jack, who was still tied to the centre mast. Barbossa hurriedly tried to regain his composure, but it was too late. Jack had witnessed the exchange and he knew what it meant.

"Smyth? Didn't we once know someone named Smyth? Don't tell me," Jack said, pretending to work through it. "I'm remembering the visage of a pretty young lass with one undeniable flaw – you. Ah, yes, that's it." He was undeterred by the snarl on Barbossa's face. "Margaret Smyth. I can picture her as if she were standing in front of me!"

Jack's eyes went to Carina, her face cast in moonlight as she studied the stars and adjusted the ship's course.

"I do wonder how someone as hideous and ugly as you could produce a fetching creature such as that," Jack said in mock puzzlement. "I know mirrors are hard to come by at sea – but you truly are unsightly."

Barbossa grabbed Jack by the throat. "Margaret died and I summoned as much honour as a worthless blackguard ever could," he hissed. "I named the nursling myself. Placed her on the orphan steps, never to see her again. I thought the ruby would afford her some ease of life. But I never imagined she'd take those scribblings and make a life from it – a life that would lead her back to me!"

"Shall we make an accord," asked Jack, "or should I tell Carina Smyth what we both know to be true?"

Barbossa was fuming. Carina had such grand visions of her father, he knew it would devastate her to learn what kind of man he really was. "Tell me what you want!"

"Well, let's see," Jack said, cocking his head. "I want my compass, your jacket, a lock of your hair, two hundred and sixteen barrels of rum ... and the monkey."

"You want the monkey?" asked Barbossa. The two Jacks had never got along.

"Yes," replied Jack, "for dinner. And throw in the Trident if you don't mind. Everyone else seems to want –"

The monkey reached for a rag and stuffed it into Jack's mouth.

"No deal, Jack," said Barbossa. "A clever girl such as that would never believe a swine like me could be her blood. The Trident will be mine."

"*Redcoats!*" Henry called, descending from the lookout. Barbossa rushed to the rail to see the *Essex* bearing down on the *Black Pearl*.

"We'll fight to the last!" the captain shouted. "The *Pearl* will not be taken from me again!"

On a longboat between the two ships, Jack's crew rowed frantically in the dark, hoping to slip away from the *Essex* unnoticed.

"The *Black Pearl*!" Gibbs exclaimed, gazing out on a sight he never thought he'd see. "She sails again!"

The *Pearl* would sail for only a short time if Scarfield had his way. Thirty cannons were lit up to strike fatal blows. Nobody would stop him from obtaining the Trident and finally achieving the glory that was his due. With a weapon like that, he'd surpass any officer in the navy. Indeed, he would be more mighty than the king himself.

"Only one man will hold the power of the sea," Scarfield said aloud.

It was not to be him, though. Behind the lieutenant, the *Silent Mary* approached.

Slowly, Scarfield turned around. The skeletal hull of Salazar's ship opened up like the jaws of an immense hungry beast – wider and wider until Scarfield could see a gaping gateway from this world into the next.

In an instant, the *Silent Mary* tore through the *Essex*, snapping the once mighty ship in two as if it were a piece of straw. Explosions of gunpowder burst through all the portholes, and a great blaze of white-hot flames rose up the masts. Thousands of tiny pieces of ash that had once been a ship and its crew billowed up in the air and down into the sea.

Barbossa stared at the devastation and the fast-approaching *Silent Mary*, advising Carina, "Whatever happens, stay your course!"

Reaching the *Pearl*, Jack's crew climbed up, but those on board were too busy preparing for battle to pay them any mind. Then it was time: the *Silent Mary* was upon them.

Captain Salazar, followed by his ghastly crew, leaped onto their deck.

"We've come with the butcher's bill," snarled Salazar. "Where is Jack the Sparrow?"

Barbossa drew his sword. "We will fight to the last!"

With the exception of a few pirates who threw themselves into the sea in panic, Jack's crew and Barbossa valiantly defended the *Black Pearl*. Sadly, most did so to their peril. The ghosts had more speed and manoeuvrability. And they were already dead, so at best they could be delayed – not stopped.

Henry darted through the melee to Jack's side. As irritating as Jack was, Henry couldn't leave him defenceless.

"You've come to save me again?" Jack asked incredulously after Henry took out his gag and began to untie him. "Have you learned nothing?"

Henry stuffed the gag back in but cut Jack loose. Then he dived under the mast and swung his sword through and around the countless ghosts that writhed between him and Carina. Skilled as he was at fighting, the creatures were impossible to subdue. They had strength to attack but no substance for retaliation.

"Where is he?" roared Salazar.

Mullroy cowered in fear and pointed to the central mast. Salazar stalked over only to discover the severed ropes. He bellowed in rage.

"There is nowhere to hide!" Salazar spun in a circle, scanning the ship for a sign of Jack.

As a giant wave dipped the *Black Pearl*, Jack swung away from a high yardarm – towards the *Silent Mary*. Landing on the tip of a cannon, he twisted to look back, his eyes meeting Salazar's. With a shout, Salazar leaped to land on the next cannon. They crossed swords, their blades ringing out like a bell.

"I will break you this time," said Salazar. "I will

punish you for the pain I must endure – feeling my own death, over and over."

"Or you could simply forgive me," suggested Jack, flashing one of his signature devilish grins.

The two ships were now side by side. Jack jumped from cannon to cannon, ship to ship, using them like stepping stones over a stream, but Salazar stayed with him. They parried back and forth, neither gaining the upper hand.

The dead were everywhere on the *Black Pearl*. The remaining pirates fought on in a vain attempt to postpone their inevitable demise.

Throughout the battle, Carina strained to concentrate on the seas and stars. The time was closing in, the sky lightening in the east as the Sun began to rise. Soon she would lose the stars that guided her. Barbossa stood at her back, fighting to keep the ghosts away from her – until his peg leg slipped and was caught between two planks.

He cried out in pain as a sword grazed his side. Carina swung around and swiftly freed his leg as their eyes met briefly. Then she went back to the wheel and Barbossa resumed fighting – fending off swords from multiple attackers.

Jack, meanwhile, seemed to be out of cannons to hop on, as he was perched on the most forward cannon of the *Silent Mary*.

"You took everything from me," Salazar said, glowering at Jack from just a cannon's length away. "Made me more repulsive than any pirate!"

"That's not necessarily true," Jack replied, waving his non-sword-wielding hand. "Have you ever met Edward the Blue? He's very repulsive. The way he eats –"

Jack's words were cut off by a strange sound. It was the *Silent Mary* itself – or at least the huge figurehead at its bow. Also a ghost, she pulled away from her spot and climbed backwards towards Jack. Towering above Jack, she peeled her lips back in a horrifying grimace, ready to obliterate the pirate.

"That's very strange," said Jack of the ghostly lady. In all his years of fighting, he'd never faced off against an animated figurehead.

As the *Black Pearl* slid closer, Jack leaped away from the two ghosts pursuing him, hopping back along the ships using the same zigzagging route beneath the cannons. This time, however, Salazar lit the cannon across from Jack. Facing his death in a very literal way, Jack stared directly down the barrel, about to lose his head.

Yet with a graceful swing, Jack was able to flip the cannon around so that it fired at the figurehead, temporarily slowing her down. But it did not stop her.

Now Jack was trapped: Salazar and the figurehead were each one stroke away from finishing him.

They would have done just that had the *Black Pearl* not suddenly collided with the *Silent Mary*. The figurehead was crushed, and Jack was flung back to the deck of his ship, which had perhaps come to his aid when he needed it the most.

Bleeding from his side, Barbossa could not hold the ghosts off for much longer, but he had done well enough until reinforcements could arrive in the form of Henry.

Carina pointed at the dawn sky as he reached her side. "Henry, look!" she exclaimed as an island – really more of a large black-rock beach – became visible. "The X in the middle of the sea!"

Salazar stood above Jack, his sword raised for a final blow, when Lesaro shouted, *"Land!"*

They would soon be on the shore, where Salazar and his men could not follow. The furious ghost swung his sword at Jack.

Salazar's blade was within inches of Jack's throat when Carina sailed the *Black Pearl* straight onto the beach. With piercing screams, ghosts began bursting and disintegrating at the front of the *Pearl*. The remaining ghosts scrambled back to the *Silent Mary*.

Salazar began to retreat as well, a menacing snarl on his face. The ghoulish captain made a last-minute grab for Carina, but Henry bravely dived between them. Salazar took hold of Henry instead and dragged him back to the *Silent Mary* with him.

Carina squeaked in dismay and rushed to the rail, stretching out her hand to Henry. He tried to reach back, but their fingers missed by inches. The *Silent Mary* veered away from the *Black Pearl*, taking Henry with it.

"*Carina!*" Henry called out in despair and longing as they looked at each other, perhaps for the last time.

"Henry!" shouted Carina. She spun to face the men on the *Pearl*. "We have to go back for Henry."

Barbossa put a hand on her shoulder. "The Trident is the only thing that can save him now."

it, but it wouldn't budge.

Ssssffftt! A plume of scorching hot steam shot out from a crack in the rocks beneath the pirate. The crack grew larger; then a powerful vacuum sucked the poor pirate into the island forever.

Frozen in place, the others stared at the empty space where the pirate had stood, the diamond he'd been wrestling with twinkling as the sky grew brighter.

"Back to the ship!" Gibbs screamed. The pirates were gone from the beach as fast as they had arrived.

With the Sunrise, the huge swath of diamonds shone with an overpowering intensity.

"Look at it, Jack," said Carina. "It is the most beautiful thing I've ever seen."

"Yes," he said, "beautiful rocks – that kill for no reason." He hated when precious jewels were guarded by supernatural forces. It made for so much extra hassle to extract them.

"Not rocks, Jack," said Carina. "Stars."

She climbed from the ship and continued, "Stars and planets as they appear in the sky. This island is a perfect reflection."

"But it's still rocks," insisted Jack as he and Barbossa followed Carina along the dark island surface. "Murderous rocks."

Spellbound, Carina walked along the island, feeling as though she were treading on the stars themselves. Here were all the formations she'd spent years studying – except one star was missing. A swell of excitement ran through her as she hurried towards the empty spot, knowing just what she needed to do.

Barbossa and Jack caught up to Carina, who had found a cluster of rubies matching the formation in the diary exactly. They glowed brightly, with the glaring exception of the gem at the centre. That one seemed much duller than the others, as though it didn't belong.

Barbossa held out the ruby. "Finish it, Carina," he said.

Holding the ruby, Carina intoned, "For my father."

"Aye," said Barbossa, his face conflicted. "For your ... father."

The ruby took effect immediately. Light began to shoot across the constellation, forming the shape of the Trident.

There was an immense rumble. A crack opened in the rocks at Carina's feet. Jack managed to get hold of her before she was scalded by the impending steam. They both ducked to the side. Barbossa, caught on the other side of the crack, retreated hastily to the *Pearl*.

A sharp wind sliced across the ocean's surface, pushing the waves apart. Like an invisible sword, the wind split the ocean in two, a wide chasm gaping before them and exposing the ocean floor. The two walls of water were held in suspension by an invisible force.

As the crack beneath their feet widened, Jack and Carina slid down the side of the island, landing at the bottom of the canyon. Fish of all shapes and sizes dropped from the walls as the gap in the ocean continued to open, revealing wrecked ships and coral reefs.

Jack spotted Carina's diary on the sand and picked it up. Before he could hand it to her, Carina cried out in awe.

"Jack, there it is!"

He followed her gaze to see a giant tower

of coral twisted with sea glass rising from the ocean floor. A shell-shaped chamber lay at the heart of it and nestled within the shell pulsed the ancient Trident of Poseidon. Three wickedly sharp prongs caught the light and the weapon exuded a dangerous power.

Jack and Carina started forward.

"Jack!" A familiar voice called.

Carina spun in joy. Henry was striding towards them, uninjured and alive. "Henry!" she cried, racing to meet him.

But Henry's arm came out and pushed her aside as if she were an irritating fly to be swatted away. With his other hand he drew his sword and swung it down towards Jack.

Stepping nimbly backwards at the last moment, Jack evaded the strike. He pulled out his dagger and held it aloft, facing off against Henry. Something was very wrong here.

"Arm straight, shoulders square, front leg bent," Jack noted, his mind whirring. He'd seen enough of the supernatural to believe anything was possible.

"Henry doesn't hold a sword like that," Jack said. Darting forward, Jack nicked Henry's arm with his dagger and then danced out of the way. Henry glanced at the cut, both fascinated and appalled at the blood welling up from the wound.

"Cut me and you cut the boy," he said, turning eyes full of hate on Jack.

"Pretty sure that's not Henry," Jack told Carina.

As the form of the young boy charged at him, sword swinging with military expertise, Jack ducked and spun, scrambling to stay out of reach.

"Definitely not Henry!" he shouted.

It might have been Henry's body, but it wasn't his mind. Salazar had taken possession of him. Now the ghost could use the mortal form to exist on land, kill Jack and take the Trident for himself.

Hard as it was to accept the idea of a magical body-swap, Carina couldn't deny that Henry would never attack Jack. On top of that, Jack was right, Henry didn't have the kind of swordsmanship his body was displaying now. Still, she couldn't bear to see him get hurt, and while Jack may not want to hurt Henry, he wasn't about to let a possessed lad run him through.

Perhaps the Trident could free Henry. Carina rushed towards it.

Behind her, Salazar as Henry thrust his sword at Jack, forcing him backwards. Jack stumbled over some coral and Salazar was able to knock his dagger away. Unarmed, Jack darted away, but Salazar pressed him towards the walls of water. Beyond the border, Jack could see the silhouettes of Salazar's crew, waiting to grasp him as Salazar advanced from the other side.

"Leave him," Carina's voice demanded. "Drop your sword!"

Salazar and Jack turned to see Carina holding the Trident of Poseidon, the two-metre long weapon dwarfing her.

Henry's body pivoted and slowly walked towards the young woman.

"Carina." Jack's voice held a warning. The man before her was not her friend and would not hesitate to harm her.

She tried to hold the Trident steady, its points stabbing towards Henry's chest, but as he drew nearer, she found herself searching his face for some flicker of the man she cared for.

"Henry, please," Carina pleaded. She wanted him to stop this madness, to back away, to be himself again. The Trident dipped slightly as she wavered.

Salazar lunged forward, wrapping Henry's hand around the Trident and yanking it away from her. Carina fell back, her emotions in a jumble as she watched Henry spin in elation, the Trident cutting through the air with a sizzle.

"It's over, Jack!" Henry's voice cried in triumph as he pointed the weapon at the pirate.

As he raised it above his head, a fierce wind howled and the walls of the sea rose higher into the sky, magic flowing down the Trident through Henry and shaking the ground around them.

Carina gasped in horror as the spirit of Salazar stepped out of Henry's body. Henry crumpled to the seabed, unconscious, as the ghostly captain faced Jack. "*Hola*, Sparrow," he said.

Held tight in his hands was the Trident of Poseidon. The sea belonged to him.

CHAPTER SEVENTEEN

WITH A WICKED GRIN ON HIS FACE, CAPTAIN Salazar held out the Trident as if it had become an extension of his arm. Jack was lifted weightlessly off the ground. With a whisk of the Trident, Salazar sent him slamming against a rock – and again, and again, many excruciating times.

Carina rushed to Henry's side and tried to revive him.

"Henry!" screamed Carina, shaking him. "Wake up!" No answer.

Salazar continued to toss Jack around the ocean floor like a rag doll. *This is just the beginning,* he thought. *I am going to take him apart, piece by piece. Squeeze every insolent, sarcastic ounce of life from this piece of dirt. He must suffer as I suffered.*

Inside the water wall, the ghosts of the *Silent*

Mary taunted Carina. Since they were still dead and could not cross to her, she simply sneered at them. She scooped some water from the wall and splashed it over Henry.

"Wake up!" she cried. "He's killing Jack!"

Salazar was throwing Jack inside the water walls and forcing him back out again, half-drowned. With a horrifying thump, Jack landed hard at the base of a massive – and razor-sharp – coral formation.

Henry awoke, at first doubting he truly was alive as Carina's face gazed down at him. Surely he was imagining it. As she helped prop him up and pointed at Salazar, wielding the Trident, Henry accepted it as real. Seeing the amazing power of the Trident, he said weakly, "The power of the sea...."

"'To release the power of the sea ...'" Carina recited, "'... all must ... divide'!"

Both of them solved the riddle at the same time. The Trident held the power, and every curse was contained inside. To divide it meant to break the Trident itself!

Jack got to his feet, more delirious than he had ever been in his life. "Surrender to me now," he said to Salazar, just as he had when he was 12 and taunting him from the crow's nest, "and I'll let you live."

"You want *me* to surrender?" Salazar said, laughing. The most powerful weapon in the world lay in his hand; there was nothing Jack could do to stop him.

"I would highly recommend it," was the answer.

"This," said the vengeful captain, "is where the tale ends!"

Henry scrambled to his feet – just in time to see Salazar plunge the tip of the Trident into Jack's chest.

"No!" Carina screamed.

Jack clutched the ancient spear and stared at Salazar, who held fast to the other end.

Salazar hissed with pleasure, "Jack Sparrow is no more."

To everyone's astonishment, Jack rallied, pulling open his bloody shirt pocket. There was the tip of the Trident – lodged in the centre of the diary!

"Be the last to die, mate!" Jack reminded Henry.

Salazar grasped the Trident, trying to pull it back and finish the job, but Jack held on with more strength than he should have had, preventing

Salazar from driving it forward or yanking it back. They were locked in a stalemate.

Racing across the sand, Henry swung his sword down squarely on the Trident between the two men – making a cut as clean as the one through the liquid canyon walls surrounding them. A shock wave slammed over them all, throwing Salazar, Jack and Henry to the ground.

As they got to their feet, Jack probed at the wound on his chest, feeling it heal. Salazar, too, was whole again, the gap in his head filling in, colour returning to his cheeks, and his uniform looking newly-pressed. He was no longer a ghost, but the same man he'd been before he sailed into the Triangle. His crew stepped from the water, no longer prisoners of death.

"The curse is broken," Henry gawked in amazement. Hope soared through him. Somewhere across the ocean, his father might be free now as well.

"All curses are broken!" Jack exclaimed. "Which means my luck has returned."

Almost mocking him, the walls of water began to tremble at that moment, the sides of the canyon caving in.

"Maybe not," Jack muttered.

Preoccupied with their resurrection, Salazar and his crew did not at first see the danger.

"We are flesh and blood," Salazar marvelled. He drew in a deep breath, filling his lungs with the sting of salt air. He turned to his men, then noticed the walls were giving way, about to drown him and his men just as they got their lives back. "No!"

Above them all, the *Black Pearl* could be clearly seen sailing on the rim of the parted ocean, which was starting to fill in again. An anchor dropped from the ship, Barbossa hanging from the end, his hand stretched out towards Carina.

"Hurry!" he shouted.

Jack, Carina and Henry made a mad dash for Barbossa and the anchor.

Leaping up, the trio managed to grab hold of the anchor and clamber up next to Barbossa – but the suction of the collapsing sea kept pulling them all down. They strained to climb higher along the chain while the crew on deck struggled to haul up the anchor. The weight of too many people and the force of a swirling current were holding it down.

Soon the sea would close around them completely.

"She's giving way!" Henry shouted as the *Black Pearl* began to tip.

Salazar and his men reached the anchor and began to climb rapidly. Suddenly, the *Pearl* dipped and Carina, under Jack, Henry and Barbossa, slipped and started to fall. Barbossa's hand lunged out and grabbed hers.

"I've got you!" he cried.

Dangling over the sea floor, Carina could see Salazar and his men closing in on her. She looked up at Barbossa, and then she saw it: a cluster of five stars was tattooed on his arm. They were the same five stars that adorned the diary her father had left her. In an instant, she realized the truth.

"What *am* I to you?" she asked him, grabbing the chain to pull herself higher and closer to him.

Salazar was now within striking distance, dagger in hand. Barbossa stared at Carina, eyes clear. His expression softened.

"Treasure," he answered. *A treasure worth dying for,* he thought.

There was a flurry of motion. Jack dropped his sword just as Barbossa let go of the anchor, his eyes on Carina. Falling towards Salazar, Barbossa caught Jack's sword.

Now that the Trident was broken, the once dead captain and his crew were vulnerable. Barbossa twisted in midair and ran Salazar through for good. Carina's father destroyed more of Salazar's men as he plummeted towards the ocean floor, carrying the remainder of them with him.

The sea closed in on the gallant old buccaneer as he reached the bottom, but Hector Barbossa was at peace. In his last moments, he was no longer just a pirate. He was a father. He knew he had found more than he deserved.

Carina, Jack and Henry watched helplessly as the sea converged on the body of Captain Barbossa. They didn't have time to mourn, though, as the water crashed around them. Henry grabbed hold of Carina and pressed her to his side as the anchor rose through the waves.

The crew of the *Pearl* hauled the chain as fast as they could against the tide. Finally, the anchor reached the surface and scraped along the side of the *Pearl*. Coughing and out of breath, Henry, Carina and Jack dropped onto the deck.

Jack rolled to his feet first and walked to the rail.

The darkness was lifting over a perfectly calm sea. At that moment, the Sun glinted behind the clouds. The ocean was restored.

The crew gathered next to him and looked over the side. They took a moment to pay their respects to Captain Barbossa.

Jack removed his hat, the memories of adventures with his old friend and nemesis running through his head.

For the first time, Jack couldn't think of a clever thing to say.

"A pirate's life, Hector," he said softly.

Henry, standing with Carina, realized he had been holding on to her all that time. With great effort, he stepped away, for propriety's sake. Carina didn't seem to notice, her eyes on the gently lapping waves. Her life's questions had been answered by a single act of love and valour.

"Are you all right?" Henry asked her.

"For a moment, I had everything, Henry," she said, "only to lose it again."

Henry handed her Galileo's diary and gently

took her other hand. "Not everything, Ms Smyth."

Carina turned to him. Realizing just how much Henry had come to mean to her, she held him tight, thankful he had been spared.

"Barbossa," she said, a hint of a smile playing on her lips. "My name is Barbossa."

CHAPTER EIGHTEEN

IT WAS SUNSET AS HENRY AND CARINA, SAFELY back on land, looked over the bluffs. Gazing at Carina by his side, Henry felt a swell of happiness.

"Maybe Jack was right," he said.

"About what?" she asked.

"The unscratchable itch."

As Carina turned to him, he slowly leaned in to kiss her. With a sharp slap, she stopped him. Henry blinked at her, taken aback. Had he misjudged their relationship that badly?

"Just making sure it's truly you," she said, a smile tugging up the corners of her lips.

"It's me," he assured her, sweeping her into his arms for a passionate kiss.

They broke apart briefly, both giddy and out of

breath. Henry was about to kiss her again when he spotted a small dot on the horizon behind her. Lifting his spyglass, he saw a ship silhouetted against the deep red Sun.

"The *Dutchman,*" he whispered.

Aboard the fabled ship, Will Turner stood on the deck, his face clear and his eyes bright as he looked towards home.

Henry and his father met on the cliffs. Will held his son tight, no longer afraid for his safety – no longer a prisoner of death and despair. This was a moment Will had been sure he had lost for all time. Yet because of his son – the boy who had believed when no one else would – it was really happening.

"How did you do it, Henry?" he asked. "How did you save me?"

"Let me tell you a story," Henry said, "a tale of the greatest treasure any man can hold...."

Will looked at his son, and the living world spread out for miles beyond him. "That's a tale I'd like to hear," he said.

* * *

From the back of the *Pearl*, Jack watched the reunion

through his spyglass. "Truly a revolting sight," he groaned.

"Captain Jack Sparrow on deck," shouted Gibbs.

The captain of the *Black Pearl* strode by his crew as they offered congratulations and good wishes. These were the men who had cheated death and lived to tell the tale. This was a captain whose luck had clearly changed and who had brought them through many a danger. There was only one thing left to do.

"Bring me the monkey!" ordered Jack.

Jack the monkey jumped down in front of Jack the captain and offered the compass.

"What be our heading, sir?" asked Gibbs.

"We shall follow the stars, Mr Gibbs," said Jack. "I have a rendezvous beyond my beloved horizon."

With the monkey perched on his shoulder, Jack Sparrow looked down and watched the needle on the compass. He repeated the wish that made adventures like these possible.

"The pirate's life."

THE END

The legendary Trident of Poseidon,
said to give its bearer total control over the seas,
is being sought by three people. Henry Turner
wants the Trident in order to free his father from
a terrible curse. Carina Smyth believes it's the
key to unravelling the mystery of her past.
And Captain Jack Sparrow needs it to defeat
a ruthless old enemy, the ghostly Captain Salazar.

When this unlikely trio team up, it's a race against
time to find the Trident, or face certain death.
But their quest may be doomed from the start....

£5.99

ISBN 978-1-4748-7217-1

9 781474 872171

S48076